Touching

Cyborg Seduction - Book Four

By Laurann Dohner

Touching Ice

by Laurann Dohner

What can go wrong overseeing a bunch of android sex bots on an automated whorehouse in deep space? Great job, if Megan doesn't die of boredom. Then she catches sight of the sexiest male she's ever seen. On her grainy security monitor, she watches all his sexual exploits with the bots, and fantasizes. But that's all she can do because he's a cyborg. Then fate steps in.

There's a crash and Megan must escape or die. The cyborgs are rescuing the sex bots — taking them onboard their ship. She knows cyborgs hate humans. They'll kill her if she asks for help so she devises an insane plan — pretend to be the most realistic sex bot ever made.

His name is Ice, and Megan is now his personal sex bot. He will satisfy every sexual fantasy she's ever had — and as many more as she can dream up. She just has to figure out how to keep her big, sexy cyborg from discovering that she is all woman.

Cyborg Seduction Series

Burning Up Flint

Kissing Steel

Melting Iron

Touching Ice

Steeling Coal

Redeeming Zorus

Taunting Krell

Haunting Blackie

Loving Deviant

Seducing Stag

Touching Ice

Copyright © August 2016

Editor: Kelli Collins

Cover Art: Dar Albert

eBook ISBN: 978-1-944526-71-9

Chapter One 6

Chapter Two...25

Chapter Three 44

Chapter Four 60

Chapter Five 73

Chapter Six..99

Chapter Seven 121

Chapter Eight..138

Chapter Nine 153

Chapter Ten...165

Chapter Eleven 178

Chapter Twelve 195

Chapter Thirteen 212

Chapter Fourteen 232

Chapter One

The female voice had a high-pitched Southern accent that grated on Megan's last nerve. Whoever the programmer had been who had last worked on the station had obviously been a man with a sick, twisted sense of humor since he'd given the computer the most annoying voice he could download. He'd also had a thing for teaching Clara—the computer that ran *Folion*—how to be a smartass. Because of the state-of-the-art, artificial-intelligence chips that made up the computer's "brain", it was capable of learning.

"You have committed violations since the ship arrived at dock six, sugar."

"I keep telling you to stop calling me that. My name is Megan."

"Don't get your panties in a bind."

"I could take you offline for maintenance, you know."

The computer went silent for a few seconds. "That would be another violation. I'm keeping track."

"Bite me, Clara."

"I don't have teeth, sugar, or I might be tempted. Is it that time of the month?"

Oh yeah, Megan thought. *If I ever meet the guy who had this job before me, I'm going to kill him for screwing up a perfectly good computer.* She took a deep breath as she counted to ten. It didn't help cool her temper by much but at least she wasn't ready to try to escape the employee quarters and travel three decks to yank out Clara's motherboards.

Her attention returned to one of the screens where the sexiest man she'd ever seen slowly dressed. *It should be a crime to cover up that perfect, dusky-gray body*, she decided. He was unlike anything she'd ever seen and her one bright spot in a dismal job working as the programmer on *Folion*. She'd been desperate enough to transfer to a floating whorehouse in space four months ago since she'd needed the higher salary to pay off debts. No one had told her she couldn't leave the employee quarters, couldn't interact with other living beings, or that she'd have to put up with Clara's annoying artificial personality.

"It is against regulations to turn the cameras on in the client rooms. Master never did."

Megan rolled her sky-blue eyes. "Stop calling the last programmer that. He shouldn't have ordered you to do that. Why aren't you bitching about him breaking the rules? Did you screech about violations he committed?"

"He is incredibly handsome and sexy."

Megan immediately snorted. "He's probably some pathetic troll who couldn't get laid if he had a ton of credits."

"He had sex with the bots."

"There's a huge violation. How the hell did he do that?"

"He changed my programming. I am forbidden to keep records or report the employees for making personal use of the bots."

"Well, there's one violation I'll never commit. They are all female and I don't do women robots."

"They are artificial-intelligence, sexual-aid androbots. That is the official title the company has assigned them but you may call them bots for short. Master always did."

"I feel a headache coming on," Megan muttered, watching the sexy man put on his boots.

His hair was wet from the fresh-water shower he'd taken—one of the many luxuries aboard the expensive *Folion*—making it appear darker. When dry, it became a beautiful white-ash color. Most people would have just called it white but the streaks of light gray were something that Megan didn't miss. The sex bot moved across the room to smile at him. Her lips moved as she spoke to the client but he shook his head.

"The client has refused more service," Clara stated. "The man you illegally watch having intercourse with the bots is preparing to leave." She paused. "You will have to wait until he returns to violate company rules and infringe on his privacy again. You are making a habit of it each time this client pays for service."

"Shut up."

"Do you know the client?"

"I wish."

"Clarify."

The man on the screen closed his shirt as he headed toward the door. Depression hit Megan hard. Three months ago, she'd accidentally spotted the guy on a security feed when he'd forgotten to remove a gun he wore.

It had sounded an alarm and brought him to her attention when Clara had ordered him to return the weapon to his shuttle. Those few minutes of staring at that beautiful, burnished-gray face had done things to Megan that she didn't want to admit. His image had burned into her mind.

He was a cyborg, something that shouldn't exist anymore. Everyone on Earth had been assured they'd been killed off but obviously that had been a lie. *Is he alone? Is that why he visits a whorehouse staffed with androbots who are programmed to never keep records or report who visits them? A real woman probably poses a threat to his secret existence.*

"Clarify," the computer screeched.

"Shut up. I just meant that I'm lonely and the guy is hot."

"You are horny and desire to have sex with a client. That is a violation I am not programmed to overlook. I would have to immediately contact the company if you left these quarters. Not even Master violated that rule. Unless it is an emergency, the bulkheads are to remain sealed between this section and the rest of *Folion* where the clients have access."

"Who made that stupid rule?"

"Four years ago there was a hijack attempt and the programmer was extinguished when he refused to order me to pilot us into deep space away from help. Androbots would sell extremely high on the black market so we are always at risk of attempted theft. Company policy implemented the separation to protect you from harm and doesn't allow the clients to know there is a human aboard to monitor all the bots and to adjust our programming if we malfunction. All clients are told that *Folion* is one-hundred-percent automated to protect you."

9

"I'm not leaving this section. I said *I wish*. That means it's something I'd like but I'm never going to get. Besides that, he looks way too big. That bot is five foot ten and he's taller by a good four inches. I like my men on the smaller side—not too tall, and definitely not big enough to pancake me if he rolls on top."

"That is physically impossible. The male would have to weigh—"

"Shut up! It's a saying, damn it. Can't you be quiet for ten minutes?"

"I am registering an incoming, large vessel."

"Ah. Great. It's going to be a busy day then."

"Welcome to *Folion*," a sweet, female computer voice stated. "Please slow your speed and dock with port nine."

"Why can't you use that voice with me, Clara? Huh?" It totally angered Megan that Clara always used a nice speaking voice with clients. She got to monitor all verbal communications and it pissed off Megan every time.

"Hello, *Folion*," the man slurred his words. "What dock did you say?"

"Reduce your speed immediately," Clara ordered the incoming ship. "You are coming in too fast."

The voice on coms laughed. "We already started the party and now we just need some of your hot bots."

"He's intoxicated," Clara's annoying voice informed Megan. She changed the pitch of her speech. "Reduce your speed immediately. Warning. Collision imminent. Reduce speed."

Fear spread through Megan. She adjusted her chair, her focus locking on the screen that monitored incoming space traffic. She saw the freighter

10

heading right at them, not reducing speed at all. The big C-class, long-distance hauler appeared as big as the *Folion*.

"Move us out of their way," Megan yelled. "Now, Clara."

The engines flared to life, the sound a dull hum with mild vibrations under Megan's bare feet on the floor.

"Collision imminent," Clara said calmly. "Brace." An alarm siren blared to life and the automated warning went ship-wide. "Brace for impact. I repeat, brace for impact."

A scream tore from Megan as the other ship hit them broadside. The engines had moved them but not fast enough to completely avoid the hit. The impact sent her flying from her chair to land hard on her stomach on the floor. The entire deck shook and the station groaned.

Stunned, Megan lay there for long seconds. The alarm blared out sharp, loud whistles. Worse, she started to float away from the floor. Her fingers frantically clawed the smooth surface but she had nothing to grab on to as her body rose higher.

"Clara! Restore gravity!"

The computer had gone silent. The lights flickered on, off, on, off, but then stayed on. The alarm stopped as suddenly as it had started, followed by an eerie silence. Everything seemed to freeze in time for Megan and then she heard a dull roar. She turned her head to stare at the screens but they were white static. Her leg bumped something and she twisted in the air, grabbing for the desk she'd touched. Her fingers curled on the edge, gripped it in desperation, and she managed to keep hold with two of her fingers and thumb.

"Clara? Respond, damn it. Report to me. How bad is the damage?"

"I am still evaluating."

Hearing Clara's grating voice relieved Megan. "Restore gravity."

"I am damaged." The computer paused. "I can't restore it. I'm reading hull breaches on four levels. Five. Seven."

Horror washed through Megan. The ship consisted of seven levels so the damage had to be extensive. "Send out an emergency distress signal."

"Already done," Clara's voice changed, deepening. "There is a fire in my mainframe, Megan."

"Download your program to control now."

"I'm unable to transfer my data stream. The relays are damaged. Evacuate." The alarm started to peal loudly again. Clara's voice sounded the way a man with a damaged throat would—deep and gruff—as she opened ship-wide communication. "Evacuate. I repeat. Evacuate. *Folion* is unstable. Evacuate immediately."

"Clara, suppress the fire and download your core programming into the control room servers. That's an order."

The voice that came from the speakers had become high pitched, as if she'd sucked in helium. "I have control of the hull doors to open them. The employee escape pod isn't registering and is in part of the heavily damaged section. I have concluded it was destroyed. You must reach the client emergency pod on deck three. Leave now, Megan. I am unable to suppress all fires and we are leaking oxygen. There are explosions on deck seven." The doors that separated the employee area from the client areas of the ship slid open. "I have regained some system control but more damage is presently occurring."

Megan dropped as gravity returned with a vengeance, yanking her down fast and hard. Pain shot through her body from her neck to her lower back then to her throbbing knees as she hit the deck with a grunt.

"Download to control now, Clara."

"Unable to comply." The voice rasped. "System failure. Evacuate. Life support is offline. There is a thirty-five-percent oxygen loss from my readings." She paused. "I have missing parts of the grid without readings so my findings are inaccurate. It is logical to assume that number is forty-two percent with unresponsive sensors. Evacuate. *Folion* is unstable. There is a probability of complete destruction of all living beings aboard. Evacuate."

"Shit!" Megan pushed up from the deck and frantically looked around the control room. Her private room was located behind a closed hull door and the opposite direction of where she needed to go. Everything she owned was in that room but it wasn't worth her life to attempt to retrieve it.

"Evacuate. Twenty-one percent of active sensors are reading fire and smoke damage in this area. You have a clear path to client escape pod but you must hurry. A client is attempting to activate pod but I have overridden until you arrive. My systems are failing. If I lose that grid I will no longer have override option."

Megan ran. She had to jump over a fallen chair but then she entered the corridor. Smoke filled the air, an acrid smell that had her fighting a sneeze. She avoided the lifts, uncertain if they were working or not.

13

Grateful to have gravity restored, she made it to a down hatch. Bending as she panted from her mad dash, she yanked it open.

As part of her job, she'd learned every inch of *Folion*, so she knew where to go. As the hatch opened, clean, smoke-free oxygen met her. She quickly climbed down the metal ladder and found herself on deck three. The pod was just two long corridors down.

Megan bolted for it and at the bend of the corridor she nearly plowed into a bot. It turned to face her, a cold smile on its features.

"May I serve you?"

"Move," Megan panted at it.

She barely dodged the bot and ran around it, hitting the turn literally as her body bounced off a wall. She saw the emergency pod sign ahead, blinking red, fast flashes. The alarms were still blasting through the ship and Clara's automatic evacuation statement filled her ears as she ran.

An explosion tore through the end of the corridor with a flash of fire and a loud boom. Megan screamed, twisting around in mid run, and threw herself to the floor. A roar whooshed behind her as she lay there and threw her arms up as hot heat blasted above her. She turned her head, peeking up between her curved arms toward the ceiling. Flames licked along the ten-foot-high ceiling but then died. She turned her head, staring in shock down the hallway where the pod had been. Twisted metal and charred scars marred the wall, the light no longer blinking.

"Client has overridden pod." Clara's voice had become louder than the alarm, her annoying accent back. "He set a charge in the wall control pad and severed my connection to the docking clamps. Pod safely jettisoned."

"Oh God," Megan lay there, horrified. There were only two emergency pods so that had been her last chance at escape.

"Megan, proceed to section four of level three. I have locked the clamps of the ship still docked in that section. I am attempting to stall their ship from leaving. Hurry and attempt to board it. They are allowing bots passage. I negotiated with the captain to save as many units that could reach his ship before I lost the ability to communicate with them."

Panic gripped Megan as she pushed up from the floor and ran. She turned down another corridor, running as fast as she could. Two more turns and she saw three bots walking calmly through an open docking door thirty feet ahead. A gray-skinned cyborg stood there, looking grim. He had black hair and wore an all-black uniform similar to the one the cyborg she had spent months watching always sported. It had to be his ship and there was more than one cyborg after all. She hoped her cyborg had safely made it back inside his ship.

"Wait," she called out, pushing her tired body to press forward. Her side burned from running and she panted hard.

The cyborg faced her as she ran toward him. He frowned but he didn't follow the bots into the docking sleeve to close the door and lock her out. He waited and moved back against the wall as she ran past him, through the docking sleeve, and continued the last ten feet it took her to enter their cargo hold. She stopped since at least twelve bots were standing there motionless, blocking her way.

Doors slid closed behind her and she turned to face the large cyborg who had sealed them. He reached up and touched a control pad. "Let's go.

I don't see any more of them and I don't want to be still attached when it blows up."

"Affirmative," a masculine voice answered. "Releasing docking clamps now."

Megan leaned against the wall, bent, and grabbed her knees. The shuttle detached, letting her know that Clara was aware that she'd made it since she'd allowed them to release the clamps. The motion was noticeable but with her butt against the wall it just made her bump it. She slowly inhaled, trying to catch her breath. Her side still hurt. She'd kept in good shape, exercised daily, but running wasn't her thing.

"May I serve you?"

Megan lifted her chin to watch as one of the sex bots addressed the tall cyborg. He crossed his arms over his chest and a grin spread on his face.

"How long do we get to keep them?"

"I don't understand your request," the bot stated.

"At least four days," a deep male voice answered from the other side of the room. "We are to drop them off at the Hixton Station. We're getting paid good money for saving them. I wonder how much each one is really worth if they are willing to shell out that much to us just to transport them?"

"Probably a hell of a lot."

Megan stood, peering across the small cargo hold and she forgot to breathe for seconds while she stared at *him*. The cyborg she'd become obsessed with inched his big frame around the bots, working his way to the center of the room to reach the other cyborg.

A laugh burst from the dark-haired male. "I love the side benefits of this job if we get use of thirteen bots for four days."

Her glance darted around at all the taller bots near her, counting them. There were twelve in all. The cyborg had said there were thirteen. She frowned, counting them again. Her attention returned to her fantasy man as he stepped near her, close enough for her to reach out and touch. He grinned at the other man.

"I won't be complaining, that's for damn sure, Onyx."

"I bet not, Ice."

His name is Ice, Megan thought, as she stared up at him. He was a foot taller than her, putting him at six foot two. He looked huge in person, bigger than he appeared on screen. If she reached her arm out straight, she could brush her hand over his molded, black leather uniform, which displayed his immense biceps. In person his hair was even more amazing—white with very light-gray streaks that were only noticeable from close up but she had discovered that already since she'd had the cameras zoom in on him a few times while she'd spied on him with the bots.

The scent of leather, masculine soap, and wonderful male teased her nose. One of the bots, nearly his height, turned to face him as it smiled. The bots were all between five foot seven and six foot one and sturdy bodied so they weren't easily broken.

"May I serve you?"

Ice's eyebrows arched but he grinned. "It's a hard job but someone has to do it."

Onyx laughed. "The men are going to be thrilled with this job."

"We thought we were going to spend a lot of money using bots but now we're getting paid for four days of unlimited sex. I'd call that a good day for us but a bad one for *Folion*. What the hell happened?"

"A ship came in too fast. We were monitoring their communications and it sounded as though they were drinking a little too much to celebrate time off and slammed right into it. Good thing we were on the starboard side. The damage was really bad when it hit. Damn. Do you know what this means? *Folion* won't be available to us."

The grin on Onyx's face died. "Shit. I guess we'd better really make the best of the next four days. Maybe they'll send out another ship to host these beauties."

Ice turned his head and looked directly at Megan. She froze, her breath catching again while she stared into his beautiful light-blue eyes with silver streaks in the irises. He tilted his head, his full lips curving downward slightly as his gaze left hers to slowly travel down her body.

Of all the days for this to happen, she thought sourly. She wore a light-blue tank top with black sweat pants. They were comfortable work clothes but she probably looked like hell. Her blonde hair was in an untidy ponytail, which never completely tamed her wild curls, and she knew she looked like a sweaty mess from running. She didn't even have shoes. This wasn't how she wanted to meet the man who occupied all of her late-night fantasies while she lay in her bunk. His gaze rose.

"What is she?" Onyx stepped closer. "A maintenance bot? Her smaller size and chaotic appearance would indicate so."

She fought the urge to sag with relief. She started to silently pray that they kept mistaking her for a bot. Cyborgs had been deemed dangerous on Earth, the government had ordered their eradication, and if their continued existence was reported, Earth would probably send military ships to correct that fact. She'd always thought that's why their shuttle visited a totally computer-controlled ship. No live beings were present to report their visits and it was well known that *Folion* kept no records—to protect their clientele. Computers had no interest in earning rewards for snitching to the government but humans, on the other hand, did. She worried that the cyborgs would kill her, but as a bot, she wouldn't pose a threat to them.

Ice shrugged, looking away from her. "Maybe she's a defective model they use for general purposes or maybe she's a specialty item for some of the working human males who have fantasies about small females who have active sweat glands. I remember, while in training on Earth, that some of the human males would stare at human women and get turned on by their appearance during workouts. They indicated it made their dicks hard and they spoke of wanting to lick the sweat off those females."

"Interesting." Onyx inched closer to her, openly studying her. "I didn't know they made bots that small. I wonder if the simulated perspiration is flavored."

Ice's broad shoulders shrugged. "Perhaps." He grinned. "You have four days to find out."

Apprehension spread through Megan as the large, dark-haired cyborg grabbed her hips with two big hands and jerked her against his leather-clad body. His head bent, moving to the side as he lowered his face, obviously

19

going for her neck. She realized he intended to lick her skin to find out what flavor gel her supposed artificial body used for sweat. His hand slid from her ass to between her legs.

Megan's reaction was instinctive as she brought her knee up, slamming it between the vee of his tight pants, hitting his solid body in the groin. His response was just as swift as he shouted and pushed her from him. Megan hit the wall hard enough that it caused pain to shoot from the back of her head where she impacted.

"Son of a bitch," the cyborg hissed. "She kneed me."

He cupped the front of his pants as his head snapped upward. Pure rage gripped his features. His hand shot out and Megan didn't have time to avoid the blow. He backhanded her hard across the face, sending her sprawling to the deck. She lay there for long seconds, her face throbbing with pain, too stunned to move.

"Damn it, don't damage their property," Ice barked. "Maybe she's not a sex bot and is programmed to defend herself. She didn't ask to service you."

"I think we should throw it out the damn airlock and say we didn't get that one onboard," Onyx groaned. "Fuck, that hurts."

Movement from the corner of her eye had Megan turning her head. Ice crouched next to her, a frown on his handsome features, his gaze fixed on the other man.

"The computer running *Folion* probably recorded us taking it. You'd better hope it's not damaged since it hasn't gotten up." He leaned closer, his attention going to her.

Megan met his beautiful eyes as their gazes locked and then she looked away from him. "Systems are fine." She used her coldest voice as she forced her body to move.

Ice didn't move for long seconds, she could sense him staring at her, but she refused to look at him for fear he'd see something that would give her true identity away. He lingered next to her long enough for it to be uncomfortable but he finally moved.

Ice stood and turned his back to her. "You're damn lucky she isn't damaged, Onyx. They are only on loan until we deliver them."

Her face hurt but she didn't rub it as she got to her unsteady feet. A wave of dizziness hit her but then it cleared as she leaned against the wall, hoping they wouldn't notice anything odd about her. If she could just pretend to be a bot for four days she'd be totally safe on their shuttle.

"Right. I won't touch that one again but there are twelve others. I like that brunette one in the red dress. Then I think I'll do the blonde in leather." Onyx blew out a deep breath. "How about you? Which one are you going to take for the next four days or are you going to test out them all?"

Megan's gaze lingered on Ice's back. Both men had moved away from her and neither glanced her way. Ice gave his attention to a redheaded bot and chuckled. "I guess I have my pick. I think I'll take the redheaded model tonight and then pick another one tomorrow."

"Ice?" A male voice said from the speakers in the room. "*Folion* is warning of explosions. You should come to Control if you want to watch the light show."

21

"Damn." Ice quickly moved toward the doors. "Let's go. We'll pick up a bot when we know what the situation is over there. I hope the whole damn place doesn't go. It could take that company months to send another ship out this way and I don't like the idea of not having sex for that long."

Both men hurried out of the cargo area and, the second the doors slid shut, Megan reached up to rub her throbbing cheek and touched her inner lip. She looked at her hand, not seeing blood, and then noticed all the bots faced her one by one. She was the only breathing person in the room so they were programmed to look to her for orders.

"May I serve you?" they said in unison.

"That's eerie," she muttered. "I'm going to reprogram you to not do that if I end up having a job still at the end of this. Shut up and stand," she ordered them.

So Ice is planning on using the bots, is he? She bit her lip, thinking. She'd spent months wanting him and now she was on his shuttle. She stared at the bot closest to her, a model that Ice had just spent time with but not the exact one. That one remained back on *Folion*. A little voice in her head whispered, *Now is your chance.*

She knew it was a crazy idea but *Folion* was severely damaged. The company might not even send another ship out that way. They could open up a new bot whorehouse in another galaxy and she'd never get to see Ice again.

"Oh hell," she muttered. "Bots?"

They stared at her. She hesitated. If she did this, she would be risking her life and for what? Getting a chance to live out a fantasy that she'd had for what seemed like an eternity during her boring job? She'd spent four months alone and now she had a real chance at getting laid.

"Well hell, horny people shouldn't be put in this position."

The bot closest to her took a step forward. "May I serve you?"

Before she could change her mind or regain her sanity, Megan took a deep breath. "Authorization beta-four-nine-red dwarf." She spoke loud enough that all the bots heard her. Their twelve heads tilted upward and she knew they were responding to her verbal instructions. "Access recent data entry on visual memory. Target male with white-and-gray hair who just left this room. Verify target marked by raising right hand."

"Verified," twelve voices stated and one hand of each rose.

She hesitated. If she did this there probably wouldn't be an opportunity for her to reprogram them before they reached the Hixton Station. Once done, there would be no turning back. She'd lost her mind, she admitted, but that didn't stop her.

"Hands down." Their hands dropped. "Marked target is not a client. Do not service target. Verify order by raising right hand."

Twelve hands rose. "Drop your hands now please." They dropped. She was certain they had received and understood her orders. "As a learning experiment on your Nandois program I am now to be treated as though I am a bot. If asked, I am a test model and you will not tell the marked target why you won't service him. Verify with your right arm raised."

Twelve arms rose. Relief swept through Megan that she'd programmed them without being caught. "Lower hands, secure orders,

23

save, and mark orders as classified. Authorization beta-four-nine-blue star."

The bots heads lowered and they looked at her for a second before turning away. They were now reading her as one of them. Megan's heart raced. If Ice wanted to have sex, the only bot having sex with him wouldn't be a bot at all.

Chapter Two

"That is so weird," a dark-haired cyborg whispered. "They won't respond to him."

The cyborg standing next to him smirked. "He does visit *Folion* often. Maybe they are tired of him."

"They don't think or have emotions," the first cyborg stated.

Megan watched Ice shake his head. "I don't understand."

Onyx frowned. "I don't either. They are asking to service everyone except you. It's as if they are blind to you or just don't detect you as a life form any longer."

"Not to be rude," said the short-haired cyborg as he moved forward. "But time is wasting." He stopped in front of a bot.

She faced him and smiled. "May I serve you?"

"Yes." He held out his hand. The bot put hers in his and the cyborg led her away, probably to his room.

Onyx shrugged. "I don't know what to tell you, Ice. I guess you're not getting laid." He hesitated. "I'm your friend but time is wasting and you did get to visit *Folion* today. I hadn't gotten off shift yet so…" He inched toward a bot and when she offered to service him, he led her away.

Three more cyborgs chose bots and left the cargo area, leaving an angry Ice alone with Megan and the remaining units. Ice's hand lifted to the back of his neck, rubbing there.

"What the hell? Someone has it out for me, right?" He glared at a bot. "What did I ever do to you?"

The bot ignored him, following her programming to the letter, but he just didn't know it. Megan hesitated and then moved forward, gathering all of her courage. More than a little fear surged but she pushed it back. Could she really fool him into thinking she wasn't real? Bots were pretty damn lifelike and with their programming, they carried on decent conversations. They learned from clients, interacted with them, and were programmed to adapt with their artificial intelligence.

"May I be of service?" She was proud that her voice didn't sound shaky because of her nervousness.

Ice spun to face her, startled, and she stared at his mouth rather than into his eyes, watching his lips compress as he frowned.

"You can sense me?"

"Yes."

He paused. "Why don't they? Do you know?"

She thought fast. "You paid for service and then declined more."

The urge to look into his eyes to see how he took that bit of bullshit she fed him was strong but she resisted, afraid he'd recognize a real person if he looked at her too closely if their gazes met. Most clients didn't examine the bot's features, not wishing to ruin their fantasy of having a real woman.

"So how do I get service?"

She hadn't seen that question coming and had to think fast again. "You must pay *Folion* to reactivate use of the bots."

"But you're talking to me."

"I am not a…" She even hated to say it, detesting the stupid name the company had given them, but managed to get it out. "Artificial-intelligence, sexual-aid androbot model. I am a hybrid model in test mode."

Those full lips curved downward more. "Testing for what?"

"I'm the upgraded version," she lied, thinking this story wasn't too bad, hoping he'd buy it. It might explain what made her different and allow her get away with more shit than a bot would. Feeling braver, she actually looked up into his gorgeous eyes. "Would you like me to activate full test mode?"

Oh yeah, that's good, she thought.

Uncertainty made his eyes narrow. "What were you built for?"

Damn, can't the guy give me a break? What is he? Mr. Curiosity? He has a bot reacting to him. He should take me to bed, not play twenty questions. She hesitated.

"I'm a simulated human female in testing."

Shock was easy to read on his face. She wanted to add more but bots didn't talk unless they were asked a question. That little fact would be hard for her to remember to follow.

"A what?"

"I'm a simulated human female in testing," she repeated, glad for the opportunity to speak. "I'm a prototype. Would you like me to activate full test mode?"

"What do you do in full test mode?"

Maybe this is a mistake, she thought. "I simulate a human female." *He is super cute but he isn't overly bright.* She could live with that since she wanted him naked in the worst way. "Do you wish me to activate full test mode?" *Say yes, sexy eyes. Come on, open up that mouth and just say that one word.*

"Oh hell. I'm desperate. I hope this isn't a mistake. Yes. Run the test mode."

Yes! She shifted her body and relaxed from the stiff posture she'd maintained to mimic the bots and smiled up at him. "Hi, sexy. Where's your room?"

His gorgeous eyes widened and his mouth dropped open. "What?"

She took a step toward him and put her hands on his leather shirt. The texture of it was cold and smooth, just the way she'd imagined it would be. "Where is your room? I want you naked now."

Boy do I, she thought. She hadn't had any contact with another person, a physical being to actually touch, in four months. She really didn't want to think about how long it had been since she'd had sex. She refused to count her ex-boyfriend since he'd been so bad in bed that she couldn't even consider that intercourse. Comparing that experience to a hit-and-run would have been more accurate. The guy had been a thirty-second-not-so-wonder. She'd been sure that first time had been a fluke, hoping the reason was that he hadn't had sex in a while, but then he'd done the same thing the next four times. There hadn't been a sixth time. She'd dropped him and then she'd gotten the higher-paying programming job on *Folion*.

"Follow me," Ice ordered. He spun on his black-booted foot and walked toward the cargo door exit.

Megan stayed hot on his heels but tried to not appear too eager. She had to remember to pretend be a bot. She pushed back any qualms she had over fooling the guy. If he were dumb enough to believe it, she was smart enough to take advantage of it. The guy rated on the total hottie scale in her book and after listening to Clara, with her endlessly annoying conversations, the chance of listening to tall, metallic gray, and sexy sounded heavenly.

She glanced around as she followed him through a few corridors, identifying the vessel as an Earth jumper shuttle—a big one—and that surprised her. It wasn't old so somehow the cyborgs had acquired it. Since they weren't on good terms with Earth Government, she had a sinking suspicion they'd stolen it and that made her a little afraid. They were thieves, which didn't bode well for having high moral character.

She bit back a snort. *Like I can talk. I'm pretending to be a bot so I can have sex with a guy I've been spying on for months.* She pushed those thoughts back. After four months of absolute solitude anyone would be a little nuts, so she figured she could chalk her wild plan up to temporary insanity later. Ice paused by a door and placed his big hand on the scanner on the wall next to it. It read his palm and the door opened. He paused, glancing over his shoulder, and then stepped inside.

Her gaze jerked around the room in a fast sweep. Bots wouldn't care what his personal tastes were but curiosity overrode common sense. The size of the room reminded her of a walk-in closet with a bed, a wall of

29

storage, and a foam cleansing unit shoved into the corner. Even so, her quarters on *Folion* were even smaller in comparison. Her gaze lifted to find Ice watching her with a frown.

Shit. Caught. She forced a smile. "My polite response is that you have a nice home," she stated quickly, hoping that would cover her error by misleading him into thinking it was a programmed function.

"It's not a home. It's my living quarters."

"Information filed." She kept her smile in place.

He backed up a little, not that he had much space to move, and openly studied her body. "You're not as tidy as the other bots. You actually don't appear anything similar to them and there's something about you…" Suspicion flashed in his eyes.

She guessed that was his polite version of stating that she appeared messy. She'd run for her life through *Folion* to get to his ship so she knew she didn't look her best. The way he studied her had her about to break into a sweat again. *Is he wising up?* She thought fast, spun around to face the foam cleaning unit, really wanting one anyway, and stepped inside, purposely leaving her clothes on. She reached for the button to lift the doors to activate it.

"Wait!" He took a few quick steps forward. "You're still dressed."

She looked down, making a show of peering at her clothes. She lifted her chin. "Am I supposed to remove them first?" If that didn't cry "stupid bot" to the guy, she didn't know what would.

"Yes." He gave a nod and then hesitated before his hands lifted. "Let me help you."

She kept her gaze down and stepped over the edge of the foam unit and back onto the floor of his room. She lifted her arms the way a child would, her heart racing. He could totally help her get naked.

"What are you doing?"

Her chin rose. "I am waiting for you to undress me. The shirt lifts over my head."

His big hands hovered for seconds and then he gripped her shirt, tugging it up her body. The bra threw him a little, a frown curving his lips. Megan cursed silently, forgetting she wore one when bots didn't. She turned to present her back to him.

"I am fully outfitted to be human."

He hesitated but then his fingers brushed her mid back as he unclasped the bra. She turned, wiggled her shoulders, and the bra dropped. The straps slid down her arms and it landed on her feet. She looked up to see Ice's attention fixed on her breasts. Her nipples puckered from the cooler air.

"Damn." His hand rose quickly and his thumb brushed over her stiffened flesh. "You have reactive nipples? That's amazing."

She had to clench her teeth to not gasp in surprise as he played with her. His other hand rose to her other breast. He pinched that one between his thumb and forefinger, shooting pleasure straight to her brain. She didn't mean to but she arched her back a little to push them more firmly into his hands. His gaze lifted to stare at her while his hands froze.

"You have expressions too?"

Shit! She realized she couldn't hide everything. "Yes."

He lowered his gaze, both hands cupping her breasts. He gave them a gentle squeeze, feeling them, weighing them in his palms, and rubbing her sensitive skin again. The wonderful sensation made Megan's body react full force. Butterflies fluttered around inside her stomach and she grew wet between her thighs over what he did to her with his fingers. It had been a long time since she'd had someone touch her and the guy was total eye candy with his beautiful eyes, gorgeous, burnished metallic-gray skin, and his body to die for.

Bad choice of words to describe him, she reminded herself. If he discovered her to be human, he might have to kill her to protect his secret existence. He released her breasts and his gaze met hers.

"That's amazing. You feel almost real."

Almost? Oh yeah, he is total eye candy but not the brightest sugar treat in the bowl. "Thank you," she said sweetly, resisting the urge to roll her eyes.

"They made you a little cooler though, in temperature. The other bots feel a bit warmer and they made your breasts a little too soft and small. I like more firmness and more filling my hand."

She debated if she could get away with smacking him upside the head. She fought the temptation, guessing that blaming a glitch that made her robotic arm jerk uncontrollably wouldn't be believable. She resisted the urge and locked her teeth together instead and pushed back her irritation.

He suddenly dropped to his knees and she held her breath. He was tall even when kneeling, his face level with her breasts. He stared at them before he reached for the waist of her pants, gripped them, and just jerked them down her legs. He paused and then looked up.

"Not fully outfitted. They forgot to put underwear on you."

She swallowed. "I'll make a note."

He looked away from her and tugged her pants down completely to her ankles. She had to lift each foot for him to remove them, happy to not have shoes. She stood naked before the cyborg as he tossed her pants to the floor. His arresting blue gaze swept up her body again.

"Now you can use the foam cleanser. Do you know how?"

"Yes."

He backed away on his knees. "Do it then and hurry up." He slowly rose to his feet. "I'll get undressed while you get clean. I wouldn't want a dirty bot in my bed."

She spun around before he saw her anger. "I'm not a bot," she managed to say in a cool voice. "I'm a simulated human prototype."

She stepped into the small foam cleanser, turned, and met his amused expression. She froze for a second, wondering what caused that emotion and then she forced her arm to lift, push the button, and the wall came up from the floor to hide her from his view. Her shoulders hunched as she leaned against the wall, taking a deep breath, thinking, *This isn't going to be easy.* She activated the foam and closed her eyes.

Her body was turned on even though Ice had pissed her off. He'd insulted her breasts. She opened her eyes when the cleaning foam that covered her body started to melt, turning to water that slid down her body to the drain in the floor. She examined her girls. *Okay, they aren't perfect*

33

the way a bot's artificial ones are but for a real woman, they aren't bad. She shook her head and then took some deep breaths.

She figured she could totally play this off if she just didn't talk to the guy. Four solid days of sex was so tempting. He liked to play with bots before he used them so that should turn her on enough to be ready for him to take her. She worked up her courage, knowing that he would grow impatient if she didn't hurry, and put on her game face, hiding her emotions as she pushed the button. The wall slid down and she had to resist the urge to gasp as she stared at the very naked backside of one big, muscular cyborg.

Ice had the best body ever. She already knew that from seeing him on a screen but nine inches of monitor view through a flat glass panel on a control terminal didn't do him justice. In real person, his bare skin was a soft, steel-gray color all over and his rounded, firm ass was a bit beefy, just the way she loved. He turned to face her.

She couldn't look away from the front of him. He had no pubic hair but that wasn't what held her attention. His cock strained straight out, rock hard, and a darker shade of gray than the rest of his skin. He appeared larger in person than he had through the grainy camera lens. *Folion* hadn't had the best viewing equipment on board, cameras not high on their budget expenses but more of an afterthought.

"What do I call you?"

His voice drew her focus from his impressive cock up to his face. She had to swallow the lump of uncertainty that lodged in her throat. "Megan."

Eyebrows rose. "Seriously?"

34

If he weren't so damn hot she'd absolutely have to smack him, she decided. "Megan, unit prototype one," she lied, in hopes that would pacify him. The bots had numbers. "I'm a simulated human—"

He cut her off. "Silence."

She closed her mouth. She started to change her mind about wanting to have sex with him as he advanced slowly toward her since he acted a little rude. He didn't have far to go before he stood in front of her. A hand shot out and he gripped her wrist, turned, and gave her a tug. She stumbled a little, stunned at his actions, and then found herself standing next to his bed. He released her wrist and grabbed her hips. She did gasp as he spun her to face the bed.

One hand remained, gripping the curve of her hip while his other hand suddenly grabbed the back of her neck, wrapping around her wet hair and curving there. He pushed her forward, bending her over in front of him. Her hands shot out to flatten on the mattress. She experienced a jolt of fear as he held her that way and she saw his feet spread apart behind hers. His cock suddenly tabled on the curve of her ass—hard, heavy, and hot. Her entire body tensed.

"You're short," he said softly. "So, should I just fuck you right off?"

He wasn't hurting her but he held her firmly by the back of her neck and her hip, securing her in place. He had never acted that aggressive with the bots. Those he'd directed to get on the bed while he explored their bodies with his mouth and hands. He was a big bastard and if he just entered her, he'd hurt her. She was turned on but not enough for that kind of immediate action.

35

"I'm thinking I should take you really fast and hard."

He'd really hurt her if he did that because she hadn't had sex in a while. He moved his hips, rubbing the front of his thighs against the back of her legs, sliding his cock along her back and down the crack of her ass. He moved slowly, rubbing against her, and Megan had to fight the urge to struggle. Her heart pounded and her fingers clawed the bedding as she clenched her teeth, tightly clamping her lips together. No matter what, she knew she couldn't make a sound if he hurt her since bots didn't experience pain.

"What do you think?"

Fear kept her from forming a verbal response.

"Hmmm." He froze and stopped rubbing against her body. "I have a better idea." His hand released her neck. "I want you to roll over and spread those thighs high and wide open for me. I like to play with my toys before I ride them."

Her mouth parted and she took a shaky breath, relief pouring through her. He released her hip. "Do it now. On your back, legs up and spread wide for me, and close your eyes. I don't want to be looked at while I play."

Megan managed to move. *What the hell have I done? What did I get myself into? I never should have done this. Maybe I should just tell him the truth…and what if he kills me?* That thought left her silent as she inched onto his bed and rolled over, closing her eyes to hide her fear from him, and thankful he'd ordered her to do it.

His bed was soft and comfortable as she stretched on her back and blindly lifted her knees up to her chest, spreading her thighs apart. She was

36

exposed totally this way, vulnerable, and scared. Her heart pounded. Tall, gray, and sexy had become tall, gray, and scary. The mattress shifted and she tensed a bit before she forced her body to relax or risk him discovering her deception. A hand gently curved on the inside of her thigh, his thumb softly rubbing her skin.

"I'm going to play with you nice and easy," he said softly, his voice husky. "If you were real you'd enjoy this. I'm hoping that you're programmed for moans and realistic sexual reactions."

Megan swallowed and relaxed a little more. His other hand gripped her thigh and he adjusted her so they were spread a little wider apart. That hand slid up and his thumb brushed over the soft folds of the outer lips of her pussy. Her heart raced and she tried hard to remember to regulate her breathing no matter what he did to her.

Regardless, she sucked in air when his other thumb touched her outer lips and he spread her, exposing her inner sex to his view. She had to resist the urge to glance down at him, really wanting to.

"Very nice." His voice changed, going a little deeper, huskier. "Delicate and so pink. Your creators did a good job with this."

She let that comment slide. She tensed when hot breath fanned her clit. She couldn't mistake that for anything else as more warm air softly blew against her and then a hot, wide tongue licked, swiping from the sensitive skin at her pussy entrance up over the bud of her clit to the hood. He paused and then licked her again.

An image came to mind in that second—one of watching him do that to a bot last month. Megan had sat at the monitor, imagining his face between her thighs and tried to guess how his tongue would feel. The real thing turned out to be much better than anything she could have anticipated. She lifted her chin, her teeth locking together to hold back the moan that rose in her throat, and her fingers bit into her knees, which she gripped to keep her legs spread to his satisfaction.

Lick, lick, lick, pause. His lips sealed over her clit and he suckled it. The moan wouldn't be held back that time, coming from the back of her throat. He groaned against her sensitive and swelling bud, slightly vibrating. He sucked on her tighter, creating a better seal, and then he suckled again, only this time he pressed his tongue firmly against that tiny spot under the hood of her clit, rubbing it with each motion of his mouth.

Her fingers dug deeper into her skin and rapture tore through her. She wanted to beg him not to stop, feeling the climax coming, knowing she should be embarrassed at how fast the climax built, but he was that good and she hadn't had a man ever do to her what he did. He could get her off way better than her vibrator. It didn't tug and suck on her while rubbing a tongue against her clit.

His hand moved and he slowly pushed his thumb inside her pussy. She was soaking wet now and he pushed into her deep. He wiggled his thumb inside her, doing slow circles. With the extra sensation, she knew she couldn't hold back the inevitable any longer. She clenched her teeth hard enough to break them, turned her head, and came hard. Pleasure exploded between her thighs, her clenching vaginal walls shook with violent spasms and her mind was blown by ecstasy.

Ice tore his mouth away from her. She realized that as she fought to come down from the sexual high. Panic hit a little because she wasn't sure if she'd cried out or not, if she'd given herself away. She opened her eyes.

Ice rose, met her gaze, and she thought she saw a look of pure rage on his features for a heartbeat before he moved to his knees, bent over, and grabbed her hips. He revealed his amazing strength as he flipped her over onto her stomach. She lay there stunned for a second before his hands spread her thighs wide apart and she heard an odd sound.

She turned her head to stare in shock as Ice reached for the corner of the bed, grabbed a red packet, and lifted it to his mouth. He tore it with his teeth and she realized he rolled a medicondom over his cock. She frowned, holding still, wondering why he put one on since he never had with the bots. She wasn't worried about getting pregnant since the implant inside her uterus prevented it. Sexual diseases were a thing of the past unless dealing with pirates or other humans who refused to get medical checkups.

He met her gaze, anger definitely showing on his features. "So, you ready to get fucked, Megan? Last chance to say no."

She swallowed. "I want to serve you," she got out, saying the words of the bots. She did want him. She'd already come but she wanted to experience the sensation of his cock inside her.

His mouth tensed and then he gave a sharp nod. "Up on your knees then."

She pushed up, still a little shaky, and looked away from him. She closed her eyes and forced her muscles to relax as he put his legs on the outside of hers to make their hips more equally level with his taller frame.

She hoped his thick shaft wasn't going to hurt when he entered her pussy. She was really wet from what he'd done to her to make her come hard so she hoped it would help ease his entry. She tried to get her bearings to keep her cool but the guy had blown her mind with his mouth.

One of his hands slid around her hip, his arm going around her lower stomach and grabbed the other side, holding her in place and then he leaned forward, his chest coming down on her back. He used his other arm to brace as his hot body as he curved around hers. He put his face against her neck, breathing on her.

"You sure you want me inside you, Megan? Are you programmed for this? I wouldn't want to blow any of your circuits. You can tell me it's not in your parameters. It would be okay and I wouldn't be upset."

Having him hold her so close she could smell his wonderful masculine scent did wonderful things to her libido. She'd just come but she started to ache inside again, wanting to be filled by his tempting cock, needing to know how it would feel to have that big, powerful body of his riding hers. Her nipples tightened as his hot breath fanned the back of her neck.

"I want you," she said honestly.

His hand released her hip and he pulled his arm out from under her. He reached between them, slid his body along her back, higher, so his chin rested at the top of her head, and used his hand to guide his thick-tipped cock right against her pussy. He slid a little into her creamed slit and then pressed against her.

Megan gripped the bed, holding still, and then he pushed inside her slowly, breaching her body and stretching her. Sheer pleasure had her lowering her head in an attempt to hide her emotions from him.

"Fuck," he groaned. "So damn hot and tight." He pushed deeper into her pussy.

Her body took him until he stopped, fully seated inside her. She'd never been so stretched and filled before. She could feel every generous inch of him pressed against something inside her that really gave her a wonderful sensation. Her pussy clenched around him, tightened, and gripped him.

"It will kill me but tell me to stop if I start to hurt you," he groaned.

That was the only warning she got as his arm hooked around her waist again, anchoring her hips in place, and then he withdrew almost completely from her. He pushed in slow and deep again. Megan moaned from the wonderful sensations that slow drive sent shooting through her body. He stopped and then slowly withdrew. Her body had never been so alive, never more aware of the kind of bliss having a man inside her could create, and every movement he made had her feeling ecstasy so intense she wanted to howl. His thrusts increased in speed and he fucked her a little harder, the sound of his hips slapping against her ass grew loud in the room as both of them panted.

The climax hit her without warning and she cried out from the pure force of bliss that tore throughout her system. Behind her, Ice cried out too in a deep voice, hips slowing, and then pressed tightly against her ass as he jerked hard over her bent form, coming deep inside her body.

Megan knew she was in a world of shit and she'd totally blown it as she panted, out of breath, with Ice locked around her, their bodies still linked together. She'd cried out when she'd come and sweat beaded her body. He had to know she was real, no way could he mistake her for artificial anymore, but then he sighed.

"You're definitely a hybrid, Megan." He slowly withdrew from her body and stood. A hand lightly slapped her ass, making her jerk in surprise at the action, another thing she'd never seen him do with a bot. The bed moved and Megan turned her head to peer at Ice as he spoke. "I really enjoyed sex with you."

Ice moved across the room, the muscles flexing in his seriously nice ass and she saw his hand reach in front of him as he opened the trash by the foam cleanser unit. He dropped the used medicondom into it. He opened a drawer next when he turned to the wall, quickly donning on a pair of pants with a tank top.

"Take another foam cleansing," he ordered, still not even glancing at her. "I have a sparring partner waiting for exercise. I'll be back." He headed for the door, slapped his palm to the scanner, and left his quarters. The doors slid closed behind him.

Megan rolled over on her ass and sat on his bed, stunned. He'd just fucked her and walked out. Her gaze fixed on his boots on the floor and she realized he'd left barefoot. She sat there for long moments, trying hard not to let his abrupt actions hurt her feelings. That had just been the best sex of her life and the guy she'd had it with thought she was a damn bot, just an object instead of a woman with emotions.

"Well hell." She sighed loudly. "What did you really expect?"

She had no answer.

Chapter Three

Ice wanted to hit something as he glared at the cyborg waiting outside his quarters in the hallway. Onyx took a deep breath and then spoke.

"Is she a spy?"

"I don't know what the hell she is," Ice ground out. "But she let me fuck her. She refused to admit her deception no matter how fearful she grew. I threatened to really hurt her at first and she just held still for me, not saying a word. I thought her heart might explode in her little chest, it beat so fast, and I could nearly taste her terror at one point when I threatened to just take her without foreplay. She's obviously been trained well to be prepared to suffer the worst kind of torture to keep her cover."

Onyx threw back his head and laughed, one hand resting on his stomach. "I'm sorry fucking you is that harsh on a woman. As your friend, I could give you some pointers."

"Shut up. I said I threatened to hurt her but she got off on the sex. I made sure she really enjoyed what I did to her first. Then I gave her every excuse to stop me from taking her completely but she stated that she wanted me."

"There's no accounting for taste." Onyx shrugged, his humor gone. "She obviously targeted you. So what is the plan?"

Ice leaned against the bulkhead. "Go along with it, allow her to believe I'm as dumb as one of those bots she's pretending to be, while I attempt to figure out who the hell she's working for and what her end goal is."

"I think you should just kill her and end the danger to all of us immediately."

Ice shook his head. "No. She's a woman." He glared at Onyx. "I am still angry that you struck her."

"I assumed she was a bot. I had no idea she wasn't one until you told me. I didn't pay attention to her that closely nor did I even consider the possibility that she could be human. How did you know?"

"It left a mark on her skin when you struck her. I know my artificial sex toys and as realistic as they are, once she had my full attention it became impossible to miss."

"Everyone knows *Folion* is completely automated." A long sigh came from Onyx. "So you think another client identified the *Rally* and contacted Earth Government? She has to be a spy. We have been monitoring but there have been no secret transmissions. If they are tracking her we can't figure out how they are doing it but we're on alert." He paused. "Why not just interrogate her?"

Ice hesitated. "She's a small female."

"So?" Onyx's eyes narrowed as he studied his friend closely. "She obviously programmed the bots to not register you when we left her alone with them in the cargo hold and that explains why they ignored you when we came back from control. She's attempting to obtain certain information from you since she made it impossible for you to be with any of the bots. Don't you want to know what she wants?"

"Of course I do but she's still a woman and human. If she's a trained operative from Earth Government then she'd be able to take a hell of a lot of pain before we can break her and get her to talk."

"And that's a problem for you?"

A loud sigh came from Ice. "I don't think she's working for Earth Government. She really believes she can fool me and logic states they would have taught her better. They know we're too smart for that."

"Bounty hunter?" Onyx's lips curled in disgust. "What do you think Earth is paying for one of our heads these days?"

"I don't know but she's brave to go into this alone. Are we sure she's not being tracked?"

"Positive. We have been hauling ass away from Garden just in case they had a signal lock on her since you identified her as human. Nothing is following us and we checked all the other bots to make certain there aren't more humans in the group. Every male has reported in after taking them to their rooms and verified it. She's the only one aboard."

"What did the Cyborg Council say when you contacted our home world?" Ice dreaded asking that question, pretty sure what the answer would be.

"They are debating the matter still. They'll signal us when a decision has been made but they want to know who she is and if they destroyed *Folion* just to get her on our ship since she obviously has their protected codes to program their bots. Earth Government had to have worked with the company that owns them for her to get access."

"If they were working together, the company that runs *Folion* wasn't advised of her plan beforehand." Ice shook his head. "They wouldn't have agreed to destroy the thing or handed over a dozen of those sex toys to us if they had been informed we were criminals. Those sex bots are worth a fortune, probably those units costs more than what Earth Government is willing to pay for the return of a cyborg."

"But she isn't a sex bot, and if they know we're cyborgs, they also know there's more than one of us." Onyx shot a glare at the closed door. "Maybe they think we'll take her to Garden so they'll have our entire population when they locate our planet."

"Did you implement my plan?"

"Yes." Onyx looked away from the door. "We aren't going near Hixton to drop off those bots now. I have a bad feeling that there'll be ships waiting to blow us apart if they can't capture us. What is your plan to get information from her? I think you should send Gene in. He's been trained to detect human lies. He could scare the hell out of her, hold her, and get the truth from her."

"He's a last resort. I gripped her neck to feel her pulse and got a good read on her that way. Just make sure she's not sending or receiving a signal. I checked her over and examined her clothing when I ordered her to use the foam cleansing unit but didn't find anything. Of course that doesn't mean she's not implanted somewhere inside her body."

"We're monitoring closely. If a signal is sent from her, we'll pick it up, and I'll notify you immediately. Watch your throat. I think you've lost your sanity to keep her in your room with you. We could cage her while you

47

sleep or lock all the bots in the cargo area so it appears as though that's where we're keeping them when not in use if you wish. I sure wouldn't want to close my eyes with her near me. She might attempt to take you out if she's an assassin."

Anger tightened Ice's features and his blue gaze turned chilly. "If she tries to kill me then her cover is blown and I won't be easy on her anymore because she's a frail woman."

* * * * *

Megan stared at Ice when he returned carrying a large food tray. The smell of it made her stomach growl with hunger. She hoped he hadn't heard it as the door closed behind him and he glanced at her before putting the food down on the table. Her mouth watered and a horrible reality set in. With her big devious plot to get Ice into bed, she had forgotten about food. Artificial people didn't eat. She faced four days of starvation. *Shit!*

He removed the clear lid and reached for a strip of meat, touched it, and softly growled. "Damn! They didn't warm it enough." He shot her an annoyed glance over his shoulder. "I'll be right back. I hate cold food so I'm going to have them fix me a new dinner. Toss this for me, will you?" He left the room.

She sat there stunned for a whole ten seconds before surging to her feet. *That is luck,* she thought. She touched the meat and sure enough, discovered it to be room temperature but it looked delicious. She locked her gaze on the door and started to eat fast. She barely chewed, not sure when her next meal would come, and then hid the bread in the bottom of one of his drawers for later. She headed over to the trash dump to toss out the tray and used his cleansing unit to clean her teeth really well to rid herself of the food smell so he wouldn't detect it on her breath. Within minutes the door opened but she sat back on his bed when it did.

He moved across the room with the tray and sat on the opposite end of the bed, ignoring her completely. She watched him consume large amounts of food. When he finished he dumped what he hadn't eaten inside the trash and shoved the tray into the recycler. He turned then, his gaze locking on her.

"Tell me what a simulated human does."

Uh-oh. "I don't comprehend your question." She knew bot talk from working with them. "Please restate your question."

His mouth twitched. "Did they load you up on Earth history for general conversational skills with clients so you're somewhat knowledgeable?"

"No." She'd always been lousy with school and had never paid much attention.

"Do you know what I am?"

"A male." That was an easy enough one to answer without getting into any trouble. She wasn't about to tell him she had identified him as a cyborg.

"A long time ago cyborgs were created to be similar to what you are. We were just a tool for humans to use to make money and to service their needs." His gaze turned an icy blue as he stared at her. "They didn't care if we had feelings or emotions even though we were flesh and blood for the most part with cybernetics added where they wanted us to have them. They put chips inside our brains, trying to block pathways to certain areas in an attempt to kill our ability to think for ourselves."

She swallowed. "I did not know that but now I have learned."

Anger tightened his features. "They attempted to mass murder us when they realized we weren't brainless machines that would just die for them. We wanted the human rights we were entitled to but instead they locked up all cyborgs and deemed us a failure as a whole. Rather than just allow us to integrate with them, they decided we should all die. What do you think of that? If they got their hands on me or one of mine, they'd murder us on sight."

She tried hard to think of an appropriate response that would sound like bot artificial intelligence. She was very familiar with their basic programming. "Murder is wrong and killing is illegal."

He stood and paced the small room. Megan watched him cautiously, wondering what had gotten him so worked up. The mini history lesson he'd given her told her how wronged his people had been by Earth Government. It made her understand why they were so careful to avoid humans by visiting *Folion*. He paused, his focus fixed on her.

"Stand up."

She moved, feeling a little fear, but faced him on her feet. She hoped he misread her tenseness as normal for an artificial being. He tilted his head, watching her closely, and then reached for his tank top. He tore it over his head and then gripped the waist of his sweats. She watched him totally strip down to naked, beautiful skin. His particular shade of gray reminded her of something soft and smooth but his body was actually hard with muscle, his cock rock hard, jutting straight out and a little up. Her attention lifted back to his face when he stood totally naked just feet from her.

"Go to your knees," he ordered softly.

She knew the color drained from her face because she could feel it. She moved, hesitantly lowering herself, knowing what he wanted and could just pray he didn't use her the way men did a bot in this regard. Bots were designed for oral sex, didn't have a gag reflex or breathe air. She looked up his body after she'd lowered to her knees.

The anger still showed on his features as he took a step closer, his cock nearly brushing her nose, that close to her, it was big, thick, and impressive as hell. At that moment it looked a little frightening too.

"Open your mouth wide."

Megan swallowed hard, tempted to tell him the truth about being human but then rejected that idea. No one on Earth had been kind to cyborgs so she didn't want to test him to see if he had compassion for a human. She took a breath, placing her hands on her thighs to hide how they trembled and then opened her mouth a little. Ice hesitated and then his hand came up to cup under her jaw. Her gaze flew up again to look at his face as he stared back down at her.

Ice's thumb gently slid along her jaw, up, and he brushed it over her lips. "I said open your mouth wide."

Shit! She opened her mouth more. His thumb slid along the inside of her lip, lightly, and then he turned his hips just slightly, inching closer to her. His cock brushed her cheek. He stopped there, touching her in that way, and then he withdrew his thumb from her lips. He kept hold of her jaw in his palm.

"Do you do this, Megan? Were you programmed to take a male deep into your throat? It's not as though you breathe, correct?"

Does he know? Is he playing with me? Her thoughts were bouncing around inside her mind. Megan studied his face but besides anger, she couldn't detect any other emotion.

"Do hybrids breathe?"

"Yes," she whispered.

He released her face. "Perform oral sex. If I have you in my room and you're willing to do anything for me then I'm not going to waste the opportunity."

Her attention focused on his cock as she turned her head, rubbing against it since it touched her already. He was so incredibly hard that he barely moved when she did it. Megan hesitated and then slid her tongue out to trace the rimmed edge of the crown of his cock. She heard him inhale loudly and then she shifted, facing his sex straight on, opened her mouth a little wider and took his cock between her lips.

He tasted good, a tiny bit of pre-cum beading the head of his cock. It had a sweet flavor, surprising her a little, but definitely something she liked. She slowly fed more of his length into her mouth, exploring how much of him she could take as he held very still. She pulled back, nearly totally removing his cock but then moved closer again, taking it deeper inside her mouth. She tilted her head and started to suck on him.

Ice softly groaned. "You have such a sweet mouth, Megan. Timid but so hot and soft. Faster," he ordered. "Suck harder."

She did what he wanted, moving quicker and tugging on him more firmly, using her mouth to do it. Ice's breathing increased as his soft moans sent chills skittering over her skin. It turned Megan on, hearing the passionate sounds he made, as did the taste of him, and she suddenly wished he were buried inside her pussy. Her vaginal walls tightened as her stomach fluttered with need.

An ache built between her thighs and suddenly Ice shocked her by grabbing her head with both hands. She tried not to tense, expecting him to use her the way most men used bots on the station. Men would grip them and use them mercilessly right before they came. He tore her away from his cock instead of shoving it deeper.

"Slow now," he urged, then released her.

She looked up at him but only saw his head tilted back, his hands fisted at his sides while he stood waiting for her to comply with his order. She swallowed and then licked her lips, taking his cock back into her mouth. He didn't last long at all before he groaned loudly.

"I'm going to come," he warned in a shaky voice a few seconds before he did.

Megan swallowed every burst of his release, the flavor sugary and unlike anything she'd ever tasted. They may have made him humanoid but he was different from humans in more ways than his genetically altered gray skin tone.

Ice pulled back, forcing her to release his cock from between her lips. He stumbled, righted himself, and then bent to gently curl his fingers around her arm. "Stand up."

She rose to her unsteady feet and had to fight back a gasp when he gripped her arm and spun her around to face the bed. He kept hold of her as he forced her a few feet toward it and then spun her again. He shoved as he released her so she hit the bed on her back. She could only stare up at him in surprise as she studied his expression.

Why is he so angry? She wanted to ask but she didn't dare as he lowered himself to the floor and gripped her ankles, pushed them up and forced her legs apart.

"Don't look at me," he ordered harshly. "Keep your legs spread and stay still."

Her heart pounded in her chest as she turned her face away to stare at the cleansing unit. She had no clue regarding the source of what had angered him so deeply but she didn't care as he lowered his face between her thighs, released her ankles, and used his hands to spread her open to his mouth, which zoned in on her clit. His tongue rapidly licked at her in long strokes, over and over, and pleasure tore through her as she moved her hands and gripped her legs just under the knees to hold them apart and up.

His lips sealed over the swelling bud and he applied more pressure with that amazing tongue and wiggled it against the most sensitive part of her body. Megan clenched her teeth against the moans that wanted to tear free at the pure ecstasy that shot up her body straight to her brain. He had

54

a merciless mouth as he continued to manipulate her clit in fast, even strokes, and didn't stop until she climaxed hard. She cried out, unable to stop herself. She tossed her head as her back arched, the action pressing her pussy tighter against his face.

She panted hard when she gained control of her thoughts, her heavy breathing the only sound in the room. She didn't dare look at Ice but wondered if he would finally realize she had to be human. He suddenly released her with his mouth and let go of her inner thighs where he'd gripped her to keep her open to him. Big hands slid to her hips and then she gasped again as he lifted her a few inches from the bed and rolled her over.

The bedding slid against her stomach and oversensitive breasts as he jerked her toward him until her knees hit the floor. She winced from the shock of the fast motion and the pain of having her kneecaps slam into something unforgiving. His knee pressed between her thighs, spreading them, and his hands gripped her hips again, lifting her a few inches higher where he pinned her against the bed. He entered her without warning as his thick, hard cock stretched her pussy.

How can he recover that fast? She didn't care anymore how he did it as he started to move, pumping in and out of her slowly, creating a new kind of pleasure. She discovered heaven and hell as Ice fucked her. It amazed her that his big body contained so much powerful strength yet he wasn't hurting her, riding a fine line of aggression but not pain. Just the opposite of pain, in fact, and somehow the pleasure he gave her became more intense for her this time, as if his cock had swelled bigger and harder than the last time he'd been inside her.

Her mind barely functioned but the reason for the difference in feeling sank into her brain as they moved together. He hadn't put on a medicondom this time.

"I could fuck you for hours," he rasped. "So damn hot and tight, Megan. So damn treacherous, aren't you, baby?"

What does that mean? She attempted to turn her head to look at him over her shoulder but his hand released her hip. He gripped her at the back of her neck, gently pushing her face down against the mattress so her cheek pressed into it. Ice started to fuck her harder and faster, his powerful body forcing her to take more of his cock. Rapture tore through her as his hips slammed against her ass, making a slapping sound, and she didn't want to think anymore.

"Oh God," she moaned as the friction between them became so intense she didn't think she could take much more of it.

He didn't slow the pace but he released her neck. "Stay just the way you are. Don't move."

His hand returned to her hip and then slid to her stomach before it inched lower until the side of his thumb pressed against her clit. With her bent over, the wetness of her arousal and excitement coated his hand. With every drive of his hips, it pressed her clit against his thick digit. He pounded into her at a slightly different angle and Megan's pussy clenched around his driving cock. Within a minute she cried out as ecstasy tore through her body.

"Fuck," he roared and suddenly jerked out of her body.

It shocked her to have him withdraw from her pussy so suddenly and she wanted to scream out in protest as her vaginal walls twitched around…nothing. The climax had been intense but now that he'd left her body, it wasn't as strong. Frustration welled inside her. Wet heat spread across her inner thighs and it took her a few seconds to understand the source.

Their combined heavy breathing seemed magnified in the otherwise quiet room. Dread spread through Megan as she started to add up the facts she knew. Ice never used medicondoms with the bots on *Folion* but he'd used one with her the first time they'd had sex. He had just fucked her without one but he'd pulled out so he didn't come inside her, instead splashing her thighs with his release. The only reasons for his actions would be to prevent a pregnancy or to avoid catching a disease, two things artificial women never had issues with.

The color drained from her face. He must know she wasn't what she pretended to be, but if that were the case, why hadn't he confronted her? She wondered if she should just be honest with him since she suspected that he already knew the truth.

Ice slowly released her. "I'm tired. I've been up for a long time." He put space between them. "Do you need to recharge?"

So much for him knowing the truth, she thought, mentally split in half with relief and dread. She turned her head to stare at him over her shoulder. He kept his back to her though as he used his discarded shirt to wipe his cock. He flipped it to a clean side, moved forward, and cleaned her by rubbing her thighs before he pitched the cloth to the floor. Their gazes met.

"I'm fine."

Her courage fled as he gave her a cold look. She wasn't sure what else to say and now she faced another problem she hadn't thought about before she'd put herself into this stupid situation. If he was going to bed then what was she supposed to do? Exhaustion tugged at her but bots didn't need beds. They just stood when they weren't in use. No way could she sleep standing.

"I sleep very deeply. Don't be alarmed if I don't wake up easily. I just wanted to warn you. When I'm out, I'm really nonresponsive."

"Understood."

He blinked, watching her with that intense gaze. "You may rest on the bed with me."

That solved one problem for her but opened up more. She sometimes snored when she became overly tired and she was definitely wiped out. Then again, he'd just said he slept heavily. Maybe it wouldn't wake him. Megan stayed silent as he moved forward, closing the distance between them.

"Get on the bed near the wall. I always take the outside. It will be a tight fit but I wouldn't sleep easy knowing you were just standing somewhere watching me. I want you to face the wall on your side and keep your eyes closed."

He made her suspicious again but then he'd tossed out the question of her recharging. The contradictions were driving her batty. She pulled back his covers then realized she probably should have purposely attempted to spread out on the cover just to appear dumber but she'd already done it. She scooted under his bedding to the wall and in seconds his large, naked, hot body pressed against hers.

She closed her eyes and swallowed the lump that formed in her throat. Her ass was snug against the side of his hip and her back rested against his ribs as he sprawled beside her. He shifted, spreading his arms above her head and folding them behind his neck.

"Lights off," he ordered the room computer.

Megan lay there until she realized Ice's breathing had slowed and a soft snore came from him almost immediately. She relaxed completely when she was sure he slept.

\'

Chapter Four

Ice was tense even though he forced his body to remain lax. He made soft noises to fool Megan into believing he slept deeply. If she wanted to harm him, he'd set up the perfect situation for her to attempt it. He lay naked on a small bed with her, skin to skin, and he'd purposely led her to believe he shut down so he wouldn't be aware of his surroundings.

Megan moved slightly, adjusting on the mattress, and Ice turned on the camera in his quarters, using his remote uplink. The feed ran live in his mind so he could see her in the dark with his eyes closed after he'd turned on the night vision feature on the hidden device above his bed. Her eyes glowed, showing him they were open, staring at the wall she faced as she cautiously moved again.

"Do you believe she will strike now?" Onyx's voice streamed directly into the implant inside Ice's ear. "I'm monitoring from my quarters. If she gets the drop on you I can be there in seconds."

"I believe I can handle her," Ice replied, using his thoughts, which the com would translate into words. "You don't need to watch this. Why did you hack into the camera feed?"

"You aren't acting rationally about the human and she is obviously distracting you since you didn't even detect me here. I could have been anyone aboard ship. You were so focused on the female you permitted the hack. You should have confronted her the second you realized she decoyed a sex bot but instead you've allowed it to continue. It would have been more effective if you'd interrogated her instead of pretending to not know of her deception."

"I said I would handle this." Ice wondered if his irritation got across to his friend and fellow cyborg. He monitored his breathing to keep it slow and steady while he continued to make soft snoring sounds. "Disconnect the feed you've established."

"I won't risk your life even if you're willing to. I am aware that you've gone far too long on your wake cycle so I will monitor while you rest. So far she isn't attacking."

Ice considered the offer, wary of pushing back his exhaustion. He'd had two work cycles back to back and then gone straight to *Folion* when they'd docked as his last shift ended. He detested his perceived weakness at the moment but his physical limitations were showing after all those hours awake. He hadn't realized he'd been hacked, which was proof he wasn't at a hundred-percent efficiency.

"I have your back." Onyx chuckled. "I sure don't want your front since you believe sex with you is torture."

"Your humor is not appreciated right at this moment." Ice smiled though, knowing the other cyborg would see it on the camera feed. "Fine. You may monitor but don't ever hack into my living space again without permission."

"Perhaps I'm curious to see what you and the human do. I could give you pointers on how you are having sex incorrectly."

"When we are training, I'm going to hit you a little harder than normal for that remark."

Onyx laughed again. "I don't know. You're being irrational and showing weakness at the moment. Perhaps it will extend into your fighting skills."

"I wouldn't place a bet on that, friend."

"Rest. I will watch the human to make certain that she doesn't kill you in your sleep. Leave the link active so I can warn you if she—"

"Is moving," Ice broke in. "I'm on alert."

* * * * *

Megan thought Ice was finally asleep. She carefully rolled over to face him. He was really warm and obviously out of it. She hoped he hadn't been understating how deeply he slept, but when she rolled, his snoring didn't change. She hesitated and then slid her palm on his bare stomach. She loved the feel of his smooth skin and the muscles that lurked just beneath.

"Computer, lights on dimmest setting," she whispered.

She didn't really expect the computer to do it since Ice had probably locked even those simple controls from her. It surprised her as a dim light came on above so she could barely make out Ice's features.

He was super handsome and in sleep he appeared younger, softer somehow, and even sexier. Moving carefully she used her elbow to prop her head up as her hand caressed his stomach. She could touch him all she wanted when he wasn't aware of her intense interest.

"Ice?" She kept her voice low, just above a whisper.

He didn't move, his breathing didn't change, nor did his soft snores. She smiled, studying his mouth. He had full, pouty lips when they were relaxed, ones she longed to suck on and play with. Her hand slid up his abdomen, over his bellybutton, and then higher to his rib cage. She hesitated there before she inched her hand higher, placing it over his heart.

He had one—she could feel it beating strongly and steadily under her fingertips, and wondered if it were possible that he could love someone. If a man could ever fall in love with her, she wished it could be Ice, with his amazing sexual skills. She held back a snort at the irony of her situation. She had finally found a guy she wanted to get tightly involved with, stick with for a long time, and to be with him she had to pretend to be a sex bot.

She pushed back the covers to bare his chest to her view, a sight she realized she would never get tired of seeing. He had a sensual body that she longed to explore every inch of. Seeing it was great but touching was better. Her attention fixed on his nipple nearest her face, wondering if would awake him if she played with it. She really wanted to know if he was sensitive.

Knowing she didn't dare in case he woke up, she shifted slightly and reached up to touch his hair, spread over on his arm. She was careful to avoid brushing his skin. She lifted up a soft, thick lock, and smiled when it curled slightly around her finger before she released it.

"Ice?" She tried again, her voice rising slightly in volume.

He didn't budge, his snores didn't change, nor did his breathing. Megan felt secure now so she moved again, lifting up slightly, and curled her arm between them, resting her head on his bent, muscular arm instead to use him as a pillow. She placed her other hand on top of his heart again and then shifted her leg, lifting it over his warm thigh, going skin to skin

63

with him under the blankets. Her leg slid between his muscular thighs as she wiggled closer to press tighter against him.

"You're so warm and big," she said softly, inches from his ear. "You don't know how nice this is for me. I've been so lonely."

She thought she saw a muscle twitch near his mouth but when she lifted her head to study his handsome features, it appeared as though he hadn't moved at all. She put her head back down, relaxing, curling tighter against her cyborg.

"I want to tell you the truth, I really do, and I feel so bad about the lies. If I had a choice I'd just come clean but I'm too afraid," she admitted softly. "I just couldn't resist taking the opportunity to be with you when it came along. I've watched you for long time and wanted to be this close to you too much."

She sighed and took a breath. "Computer, lights off."

The room returned to total darkness and Megan closed her eyes, enjoying how warm and wonderful it was to be cuddled up with her cyborg. She'd never dare curl her body around his if he were aware of her actions. Bots, even with the highest programming, wouldn't ever crave the close contact with him that she did.

She moved her hand on his chest again, rubbing his rib cage, just touching him. She wasn't sure when she'd get the chance again, if ever. "I just wish things were different and we weren't enemies. You think that about me, don't you?"

Of course he didn't answer her, unless she took his snoring for an affirmative reply. She rubbed her cheek on his arm, still surprised that his skin could be so baby soft when his muscles were so hard. She stilled and exhaustion caught up with her.

She mentally set an internal alarm, a trick she'd had to use often to not oversleep since Clara had a tendency to refuse to give wake-up calls, and she was pretty sure the computer would dock her pay or report her to the company if she was late on her shifts. She silently promised herself that in a few hours she'd wake and roll away from Ice before he caught her snuggled up to him.

* * * * *

"She is asleep," Onyx said softly. "Her breathing pattern changed."

"I'm aware." Ice frowned into the darkness. "She didn't attack me."

"Perhaps she examined your body, hunting for weak spots to attack later." Amusement laced Onyx's voice. "She did seem interested in examining your body. You may have been incorrect when assessing that sex with you is considered torturous. She appeared to enjoy running her hands over you."

"Shut up. I'm disconnecting now." Ice took control of the link, turning off the feed to the camera, and blocked Onyx from hacking into his living quarters or his com link again.

He turned his head slightly, his jaw brushing Megan's forehead and he froze there, enjoying the womanly scent of her. She confused him. She'd been given the perfect opportunity to harm him if that was her intention but instead she'd used her advantage to caress him and whisper puzzling

65

words to him. It had alarmed him when she'd admitted to having watched him for a long time.

What did that mean? He didn't know and it bothered him. It implied she had to be a spy but for whom? Earth Government? Did she work for a bounty hunter hoping to score a huge reward for finding large numbers of cyborgs? Her soft, womanly body tempted him to touch her as she snuggled against his side and her breath fanned his arm, making him aware of her even more.

Her breast pressed to his rib cage taunted him and his hand itched to cup that soft mound that rested there. He admitted that what he really wanted to do was roll over, pin her under him, and fuck her again. He couldn't get enough of the little human and no other female had ever affected him that strongly.

He had avoided growing attached to any female. He'd seen his friends join family units, the females controlling every aspect of their lives. The women scheduled when her males got to see her, right down to when she would have sex with them, and controlled their careers to help keep her males from being near her at the same time. As a male in a family unit contract he wouldn't be permitted to touch other females. Even bots would be off limits to him, the females stating that it wasted precious sperm and lowered their count for breeding purposes.

Ice enjoyed his freedom. He needed to be in control of his career, deciding when he would have sex, and scheduling visits to *Folion* whenever possible between missions they were assigned. Attachments to females were mistakes other males made, in his estimation, and now he felt things for a human. She'd said they were enemies and that statement was correct. He couldn't trust her, didn't even know her real reason for being with him or why she had come aboard the *Rally*, yet he refused to do the logical thing. That would have been to return her to the cargo hold, place her under arrest, and allow Gene to interrogate her until she gave up every secret she kept.

Megan moved and he focused solely on her as her hand slid lower to his hipbone, her small fingers curving around it, and her thigh slid upward to rest against his balls. The soft glide of her skin against his sensitive sac had his cock twitching to life, blood rushing there, and the urge to roll her grew stronger.

Disbelief welled inside him. So did frustration when he ordered his body to ignore his physical reactions to Megan, attempting to shut down the part of his brain that controlled his sexual desire, and it refused to be denied. His cock hardened instead of softening and lifted higher, pressing against the bedding, throbbing. He tried again, mentally ordering his body to shut down in that regard but his sex taunted him by continuing to ache for Megan's body. It made it worse when her hand shifted a little lower, lightly pressing against the shaft.

He locked his teeth together and lay there for a long time, too aware of her breathing, the way every breath pressed her breast against his chest and then eased. She tortured him with her pinky pressed to the side of his cock, only she wasn't even aware of what she did to him. He wondered what type of flaw plagued him to make him act the way he had recently. Perhaps Onyx was correct in stating that he had become irrational. His control had slipped and so had his common sense. He had a weakness suddenly and her name was Megan.

Ice discovered that when his sexual need eased, he found enjoyment in having a woman sleeping in his bed. He'd never had one share a sleeping cycle with him before. Sexual encounters with cyborg females were arranged, timed, and once the intercourse completed, they separated. That had always been the case since Ice had never joined a family unit. A yawn threatened that he stifled and he allowed his brain to totally shut down so he could sleep.

* * * * *

Megan woke up to darkness, confused for a moment, and then smiled as she remembered where that wonderful source of warmth came from. She slowly lifted her leg, cradled snug between Ice's thighs, realizing that he'd stopped snoring, and regretted it when she turned over to face away from him. She hesitated and then wiggled so her ass and backside were still pressed firmly against his warm body.

Ice suddenly rolled, faced her back, and his arm wrapped around her waist. She was stunned as he spooned her and became outright astonished when she realized Ice's hard cock pressed against her. A grin curved her lips at the proof that cyborgs men got hard-ons when they slept, just the way human ones did.

A large, hot hand moved and gripped her breast. Megan's eyes flew open as Ice shifted his big body, grinding his cock against her ass. Desire flared inside her, even though she was still half asleep, and she lifted her thigh to make room for him. His cock ended up pressed against her pussy.

68

She wiggled her ass again and the body behind hers suddenly tensed as the hand holding her breast squeezed.

"Lights on," Ice rumbled, his voice gruff.

Harsh, strong lighting blinded Megan as the room brightened to full capacity. Before she could get her bearings, Ice released her, and rolled away. She thought she heard him utter a soft curse. She blinked rapidly, trying to adjust her vision to the bright lighting as she turned her head. She watched the naked backside of one sexy cyborg walk quickly across the room to the foam cleansing unit. It stunned her when he stepped inside without even glancing at her and hit the button. The wall rose, enclosing him.

She sat up and yawned, having no idea how long she'd slept but knowing it had been a few hours at least. Her body was rested and obviously not exhausted still since she'd physically responded to a turned-on cyborg. She could hear the unit working as Ice foamed up to start his day.

Do I get up and get dressed? Stay in bed the way a good bot would since he didn't tell me to move? Damn, she thought, staying put, deciding a bot wouldn't assume anything, just wait for orders.

Minutes later the cleansing unit door lowered and a very naked and still aroused Ice stepped out. His blue gaze locked on Megan and her heart pounded in her chest when she recognized that look he gave her. He slowly approached her.

"Get up," he ordered.

Megan forced her body to move and she stood next to the bed totally naked, staring up at Ice as he stopped just feet from her. Ice let his attention lower from her face down to her breasts. His tongue slid out between his full, sexy lips, and he wet his lower lip.

"Turn around, face the bed, bend over, and grip the edge of the frame now to brace for me while I fuck you."

Her heart raced, knowing for sure what he would do to her. She was ready—she could feel the wetness between her thighs still, proof that her touching him and sleeping next to him had affected her the way it had him. His proof of passion pointed straight up and out, impressively standing at attention just for her. Megan slowly followed his orders, presenting him with her ass as she bent. Her fingers curled around the edge of the bed just as he'd demanded, her palms on the mattress to hold her weight up.

"Spread your thighs wider apart."

She widened her stance by two feet and she could see between her own legs as Ice took a step closer, then surprised her when she saw him lower his body to crouch behind her, his weight resting on his bent legs. His hands gripped her inner thighs high and he gave her a little nudge so she spread her thighs wider by another foot.

"You're wet," he whispered softly.

Megan wished she could see his face but with the way he had her positioned she'd have to twist her waist to peer at him around her hip. She knew that was a no-no. She pretended to be a bot and she'd been given orders. She had no guess what he'd do to her but she really wanted to find out, certain it would involve pleasure. Every time Ice touched her he made her come.

The large, warm hand curved around her thigh moved and his thumb brushed through the proof of her desire, rubbing through her slit to her clit, coating her more and teasing her. Her eyes closed and she licked her lips to wet them. Her breathing increased as he slowly rubbed back and forth. His other hand left her thigh and then curved around her ass cheek. He slowly rose and his thumb left her. Megan's eyes flew open as his feet moved to the outside of hers and the hand on her ass curved around her hip. His cock brushed her as he used his free hand to adjust it and then he entered her pussy with one long, slow drive of his hips.

"Yes," he rasped. "If there's sheer pleasure, feeling how tight you are, how ready you are for me, this is it."

Megan couldn't agree more as he seated his cock deep inside her body, her vaginal walls stretching to accommodate his thick shaft. He paused there for a moment, his hand on her hip tightening his hold, and then he started to move. He withdrew almost completely and then slid back in, keeping his pace slow.

A moan rose that she fought to contain as she pressed her lips tightly together. She couldn't decide what felt better—Ice fucking her slowly or when he took her hard and fast. Both brought her immense pleasure as he continued to pace his hips leisurely, taking his time to enjoy the feel of them together. She knew with all certainty that she preferred him without the use of a medicondom. The sensations were better, he wasn't constricted at all in one of them, and the texture of skin against skin was heaven.

71

"Put your hands on the mattress higher at your shoulders," he ordered.

She released the edge and did what he said. Her palms flattened on the messed-up bedding and her arms locked to hold herself still as he moved against her. Ice's other hand wrapped around her as he bent over her, pinning her. He balanced his body by bending his knees slightly, and his hips moved faster, his hand bracing on her hip so she kept them both from falling forward. His hand slid between her thighs, pressing against her clit as he fucked her harder, faster, drawing the level of rapture higher.

The moans tore from Megan now, unable to hold them back as he pounded his hips against her ass, his cock driving in and out of her, hitting every nerve ending inside her pussy in a way that had her fighting to keep her legs locked. Her knees wanted to buckle, the sensations that intense from the double stimulation of his cock inside her and his thumb rubbing her clit.

The climax gripped her and Megan cried out loudly. Her elbows gave way and she found herself pressed tightly over the bed. Ice shouted out behind her right as he pulled his cock completely out of her to spill his release on her thighs then collapsing down on her back, his weight nearly crushing her but she could gasp in air.

Chapter Five

When they both got their breathing under control, Ice didn't move away. He had her pinned over the side of his bed. His thumb, still against her clit, moved though and he rubbed her slowly. She didn't think she could handle him touching her oversensitive clit but she was wrong because ecstasy shot through her system at his mere touch.

"What is your directive, baby? Tell me," he ordered softly.

She tried to lift her head but he released her hip, lifting his chest from her back a few inches, but keeping his other hand firmly against her clit. He pushed her head back down, pressing her cheek against the bed again. He held her there firmly, not allowing her to move.

"I don't understand," she panted the words, still trying to recover.

"I can do this for hours." He leaned over her so his weight pressed against her ass and his still-hard cock ended up trapped between her thighs. "I'll fuck you over and over. Tell me what you want or need from me, Megan. How much can you take before you break? I want you to answer me."

Her thoughts were jumbled with him rubbing her clit. "I—"

A bell sounded loudly in the room and Ice cursed, he straightened and moved away.

"Get under my sheets now and cover up. Someone is at the door." He sounded irritated.

Saved by the bell, she thought, shaking as she did what he told her. She fought the covers free of the jumble they were in and moved under them, covering her body as she turned to face him. Ice had his back to her as he jerked up his pants and fastened them. He walked the few feet to the door, slapped his palm on the scanner, and it swished wide open.

She couldn't see who stood there with Ice's big body in the way but she could hear just fine.

"We have company. The *Bridden* just docked with us. The council contacted them and they were still close by." The male's voice wasn't one Megan recognized. "They sent Blackie here to deal with the problem."

"That's not necessary." It was clear that anger ruled Ice's emotions. It showed in his tense body and the way his hands fisted at his sides.

"He has his orders and you have yours from the Council. He's waiting in the cargo bay with the bots not in use. He's ordered all of them returned there immediately." The cyborg paused. "All of them."

"I understand." Ice stepped back. "I'm on my way." The doors slid shut.

Questions filled her mind about Blackie. She really wanted to ask but she didn't as Ice softly cursed and moved to the side of the room with the built-in drawers and shelves. He yanked open a lower drawer, shoved stuff around, and then straightened, fisting a few articles of clothing. He turned to meet her curious gaze.

"Get dressed now." He threw the clothes at the bottom of the bed. "I have to return you to the cargo hold and talk to someone."

Unease gripped Megan while she stared uncomprehending at Ice. He jerked his gaze from hers and returned to the open drawer, grabbed out a shirt, and kept his back to her while he put it on.

"Hurry up, Megan. We need to get there now. That's an order."

She moved slowly, dressed, and kept darting glances at Ice. He kept his back to her as he bent to put on his boots, not bothering to even put on socks first. His movements were jerky and she could tell he was upset for some reason as he straightened and ran his fingers through his silky hair. His chin lowered. He turned to face her and then he stared at her with an icy gaze.

"Let's go. Do exactly what I say, Megan. Am I clear?"

"Yes." She swallowed the lump that formed in her throat.

He turned, spinning away, and slapped the scanner hard with his palm, opening the doors. He paused. "Let's go. Keep up with me."

The urge to confess to Ice about her lies became so overpowering that Megan actually opened her mouth as they marched quickly down a corridor. She didn't know what was going on or why the council, whatever they were, had sent some man named Blackie. It worried her that Ice had taken her from his room. She took a deep breath to fill her lungs for the words that she knew she had to utter. Would Ice be furious? Would he hurt her? She wasn't sure.

A door opened in front of them and whatever she'd been about to say was lost to the shock of seeing a black-haired cyborg with dark-gray skin step into the corridor. He wore all black from his throat to his glove encased hands, all the way down to his chunky, military-style, black boots. The look of pure coldness on his harsh features stunned her enough to keep her mute. He had the coldest blue eyes she'd ever seen, even icier than Ice's with his dark coloring amplifying the blue, before his intense gaze shifted to Ice.

Ice stopped, his hold on her arm making her halt as well. "You aren't needed here, Blackie."

"The council disagrees." The man had a deep, harsh voice. "Bring *it* into the cargo hold."

Ice hesitated but then nodded. "Of course."

The "it" the new cyborg referred to was her and she knew it. Ice took a step, tugged on her arm, and the other cyborg stepped aside to let them pass. Megan did a quick head count and realized all twelve bots had been returned to the room. Ice stopped just inside the door and released her. She missed his touch.

Ice turned to face Blackie as the cyborg followed them through the doors that closed firmly behind him. Ice spoke first.

"What does the council want?"

"The truth, regardless of what it takes."

"I have this under control."

The dark-skinned cyborg arched a black eyebrow. "They disagree. Step aside and stay out of this. That's a direct order from Councilman Zorus. He put me in charge of this situation and if you'd bothered to read your orders they sent you, you would be aware of that."

The rage on Ice's features clearly showed but he still moved to the bulkhead next to the door and leaned against it. Movement out of the corner of her eye had Megan turning her head to watch as four other cyborgs moved from behind the bots that had hidden them from her view at first. She had a sinking feeling in the pit of her stomach as she looked back at the scary-looking cyborg.

Blackie moved to the bot nearest him, studying it intently, and the bot responded to his presence.

"How may I serve you?"

He inched away from it to the next one, stopping in front of it, carefully examining it. The model smiled at him.

"How may I serve you?"

He took a deep breath and then he stopped in front of Megan. Her heart pounded as she stared at his leather-clad chest, not daring to look up into his frightening blue gaze. She said nothing, unable to because of the fear that had her frozen where she stood. She had a really bad feeling that they knew she wasn't a bot and didn't know how to react. She was damned either way. If they knew the truth but she still lied, it could anger them more. If they didn't know, she didn't want to risk her life by giving herself away.

Blackie's hand lifted but she never saw the blow coming since she wasn't following his movement. Pain exploded throughout the side of her head as she hit the unforgiving floor on her side. She lay there stunned, her ear ringing, and then suddenly someone crouched next to her. A warm hand gripped her hip and she turned her head, reeling from the shock and pain from the cyborg backhanding her, to see Ice next to her, glaring up at the cyborg who'd struck her.

"What the hell are you doing?" Ice snarled the words.

"I told you to stay out of this." Blackie frowned. "Move away from *it*. I'm going to get answers."

Ice didn't follow orders. He instead looked down, meeting Megan's terrified gaze, and softly cursed under his breath just loud enough for her to hear him. He twisted enough to reach for her with his other hand and she flinched as his hand curved gently around her lower jaw. His thumb brushed the side of her mouth and she heard him growl. He twisted his head, glaring up at Blackie.

"You don't strike her."

Blackie shook his head. "You've gotten attached to one of them? Have you lost your reasoning, Ice? They are nothing to us. You know better."

Ice released her and rose to his full height. "You shouldn't ever strike a woman, damn it."

"She's not a woman. She's a bot, remember?" Blackie took a step to the right to clear his path to Megan. "Move out of the way now. That is a direct order."

"Ice," Onyx warned softly. "Move away. He's here on the behalf of the council and we've been ordered to give him whatever he needs to get what he came for."

"Stay out of this." Ice didn't even look at his friend, instead he glared at Blackie. "I won't allow you to abuse her. Ask her your questions but keep your hands to yourself."

"You're fucking it, aren't you?" Amusement suddenly curved Blackie's lips. "Is it that good? If so, I'll find out for myself soon if she won't break since that's my next option." His smile died. "Don't make me order your own team to restrain you because I will have them do it. After I'm done here I need to report to the council." He paused. "Do you really want me to have to tell them that you tried to protect it?"

"She's not an "it" so stop referring to her as such." Ice's voice deepened into an angry tone. "Megan, get up." He reached back, holding out his hand. "Now."

She tried but as soon as she pushed against the floor to rise, the room spun and black dots blinded her. The dark-gray cyborg had really clocked the side of her head hard. She made a soft moaning sound as she collapsed back to the floor and then suddenly two arms slid under her. She stared up at Ice as he lifted her gently into his arms, cradling her against his chest as he rose to his feet and turned to face her attacker.

"Get me a medic, damn it." He glared at Blackie. "You injured her."

"That's the least of her problems. Put her down and leave if you can't handle watching a little blood spilled. This is too important for you to intervene."

"I won't allow you to kill a woman on my ship."

"It isn't yours. The *Rally* belongs to all of Garden."

"Today it is mine," Ice snarled. "Today I'm in command so move out of my way so I can get her medical help."

"Damn it," Blackie cursed. "You really did fuck her, didn't you? I never thought you'd honestly touch one. Is that it? Is she that good in bed that you feel the need to protect her? If she's that great then I need to change my tactics. Show me to a room with a bed and leave her with me. I'll get answers from her with pleasure instead of using pain."

"I said move out of my way." Ice's voice grew harsh, a frightening sound to Megan even though she knew it wasn't directed at her.

They knew she wasn't an artificial woman and yet Ice protected her. That knowledge astounded her. Had he known all along? She went over everything that had happened between them and realized that he probably had. He'd even fed her so she didn't go hungry when he'd brought in that tray of cold food, pretending he couldn't eat it, even leaving her alone so she could gulp it down. She hesitated and then wrapped her arms around his neck.

Ice's beautiful blue gaze flickered to hers for a few heartbeats before he glared back at the cyborg in his way. "I said move, Blackie."

"You have no authority over me." The man crossed his arms over his chest. "Put her down and leave this room. You're obviously too involved with the woman to be rational. You need to go."

"Onyx," Ice's voice lowered into an even deeper pitch. "Forward now."

Onyx moved to stand next to Ice, who turned, shoving Megan into the other man's arms to both their surprise, leaving Megan being held by one unhappy cyborg. Ice stepped away and closed the distance between him and Blackie. Ice grabbed the man and threw him hard against the doors, gripping the front of his shirt with his fists, and hauled the shocked cyborg a few inches off his feet.

"The *Rally* is under my command today, everyone on it follows my orders, and now you're on my ship."

"Ice," Onyx warned softly. "The council sent him. They are going to be alarmed by your actions and take it as a direct violation of orders if you don't stop now."

"I don't care." Ice continued to glare at Blackie. "I won't stand by and watch abuse on a helpless female. If those are the orders from a council member, he's wrong in giving them. I'm taking her to medical and then I will get the answers they seek from her my way." He released the other cyborg, dropped him to the floor, and stepped back. "That is how it will be."

Ice took Megan from Onyx, cradled her in his arms once again, and stormed toward the door. Onyx moved, slapping his hand to the panel to open it, and Ice left the cargo hold with her. Megan hesitated and then wrapped her arms around his neck, staring at his angry features. He refused to glance at her, keeping his attention on where he walked.

"Thank you," she whispered.

"Not now." He sighed. "You're trouble, Megan. Is that even your real name?"

"Yes."

He grunted. "I'm not sure I believe anything you say."

"It's the truth."

"We'll talk later. For now, are you all right?" He finally glanced at her for a few seconds before looking away again.

"I'm a little dizzy and my ear hurts. He nailed me pretty hard."

"You're bleeding." His tone turned gruff.

She licked her lips and tasted blood. She hadn't noticed that at first, too taken aback by the unprovoked attack. A cyborg waited in a hallway a few turns later and Ice stopped.

"Onyx said you were coming with a human." He waved his arm. "Bring her in."

The room appeared to be the same size as Ice's quarters, obviously not a medical room but instead the cyborg's private quarters. Ice gently placed her on the man's bed. The new cyborg brought over a bag, dropped it at the end of the mattress, and his dark-brown gaze studied Megan for a few seconds before he focused on Ice.

"Onyx informed me she took a hit to the head and a tumble to the floor. What are her complaints?"

"I don't like being hit," Megan said softly.

Ice's lips twitched but he didn't smile. "The side of her lip is bleeding, her ear on that side hurts, and she's dizzy, Varion."

"She's too fragile for one of our males to strike." The medic frowned at Ice.

"I'm in agreement."

"Then why did you do this to her?" Varion moved, pushed Ice out of his way, and bent over Megan to stare at her mouth. "Open up wide and allow me to see the damage."

"I didn't hit her." Ice sounded insulted. "Blackie did."

"He's such an asshole," the medic muttered, gently touching the side of her mouth and it made her flinch. "The cut is small but facial cuts bleed a lot. I don't see any inner cheek damage." His gaze locked with hers. "Open your eyes as wide as you can and do not look away from me. I am checking the extent of your injuries."

Megan did as he asked and then realized the guy had strange eyes. His pupils weren't rounded exactly but more squared. She frowned but didn't mention it, not wanting to be rude. She had to blink but he didn't complain when she did since she looked right at him again every time. A few minutes passed and then he straightened and turned away to face Ice.

"I scanned her. She has no internal bleeding, no swelling, no cranial fractures, or trauma to the brain. She has a slight concussion but she will be fine. It's mostly shock trauma from the blow. She may experience dizziness for a short period of time and perhaps a headache. I'll give her something for the pain."

"You scanned my brain?"

The medic turned his head after he removed something from the bag at her feet, meeting Megan's curious gaze, and nodded as he gave an injection in her arm. "I'm a medical model implanted with special features such as enhanced vision that can perform medical scans. They created me to be a medic unit." He faced Ice again. "I heard—"

The doors suddenly opened and Blackie stormed in, looking smug as he gave Ice a cold smile. "I informed the council of your behavior and they have made a ruling. They were not pleased with this turn of events. They are confident she's working alone since she's not being tracked or attempted to send a distress signal to any co-conspirators now that she's aware her cover is blown. Councilman Zorus was very persuasive in his argument due to the fact that we're close to home on how threatening the female is." The man shifted his stance as he paused for long moments, seeming to silently communicate something with a flash of his cold gaze to the other two cyborgs. "You know how Zorus is. They voted in his favor. More of them agreed with him than not."

"Son of a bitch," the medic hissed.

Megan had a sinking feeling that, whoever this Zorus was, whatever vote he'd won, it would be very bad news for her.

Ice's features hardened and he moved to the wall. He planted his hand on a panel there and it came on. He stood there with his back to the room and his body tensed noticeably. He jerked his hand off the panel and turned to glare at Blackie.

"I just read the order."

"Did you think I would attempt to deceive you?" A black eyebrow arched.

"Get off my shuttle. I just sent a message to the *Bridden* that you are on your way and they can undock with us in minutes. Go now and return to your original mission."

"I'm not leaving yet. I am to verify the council orders are followed so I will do it myself." He took a step toward the bed.

Ice moved fast, shoved Blackie back hard until he slammed into the bulkhead wall next to the door. "I understood the order and I will take responsibility for the female since I am the one who chose to take us to

Folion. I'll take her to my quarters and make her as comfortable as possible."

That didn't sound bad or terrifying. Megan relaxed. "What's going on?"

No one answered until Blackie met her gaze. He sighed. "You are going to gain your freedom from us. We've been ordered to drop you and the bots off at Hixton Station as previously arranged."

"Don't," Ice snarled.

Blackie frowned. "I have my grievances against humans but I'm not totally without sympathy. I see that you care what happens to her and that you don't want her last moments with us to be frightening. I'm not leaving until the order is followed and she's no longer a threat but I will allow you to take her to your quarters to say goodbye." He paused. "I'll have a special meal sent to your quarters so she has a good meal first. That's the most I can do for you both. It will make things easier to end this."

The tension eased from Megan's body. "Thank you. I swear I really won't tell anyone about the existence of cyborgs. I've known about your people for months and never once reported you."

Blackie ignored her as he stared at Ice until Ice broke eye contact and faced Megan.

Ice studied her carefully and then nodded, taking his attention from her to glare at Blackie again, who still stood by the door. "I understand."

Blackie's mouth tensed in a firm line as he nodded, spun around, and quickly left the room. "Don't take long."

The medic had a grim expression on his pale-gray features. "You can leave and I'll take care of her until she departs."

Ice shook his head. "I'm the commander today and my orders put us in this situation. We're going to my quarters now."

"Of course." The medic nodded.

Ice met her gaze. "Would you like me to carry you again? Are you feeling weak or dizzy still? I apologize for Blackie striking you. It never should have happened and it wouldn't have if my council wasn't afraid you were a threat to our future. You lied about what you were, which makes them wary of you."

Megan sat up slowly and realized the shot had made her a little lightheaded but she moved fine. She didn't suffer any dizzy spells or disorientation. She swung her legs off the side of the bed and then got to her feet. The room didn't spin and her knees held her weight easily. She looked up, having to raise her chin a lot since he stood so tall, just to meet Ice's concerned gaze.

"I'm fine. I can walk."

"Good. Follow me. It is just down the corridor."

Megan started to follow behind him as he moved toward the door but then she paused, giving the medic a small smile. "Thank you for being kind to me and treating me."

He froze, his dark gaze locking with hers. "You are welcome."

"Come with me, Megan," Ice urged softly.

Four doors down he paused, placed his hand the scanner, and they entered his quarters. Megan was glad to be back in a familiar setting and moved to his bed. She sat and faced him, only to realize he stayed far from her, just inside the door. The grim set of his lips had her feeling ill at ease again.

He said nothing for long moments and then he took a deep breath. "You said you knew of our existence for months?"

She nodded. "I'm not normally allowed to see the clients on *Folion* but you came onboard with a weapon so it triggered the alarm. When that happens I have to monitor the situation visually on the security cameras. That's when I saw you." She didn't mention that she'd ordered Clara to deem him a high-security risk so that every time he returned to the station she'd be informed. She really didn't think he'd meant to bring a weapon onboard or that he was dangerous, it being just the only way she could see him again. "I only got to monitor verbal interaction between the main computer and incoming ships unless there was a problem that arose."

"We were unaware that there were any live employees aboard."

"The company wants people to believe that. They had an incident where someone tried to hijack *Folion* once. The hijackers who grabbed the programmer tried to use him to steal the station. They murdered him when he refused to order Clara to move the ship into deep space. It keeps me safe from the same fate if no one knows I'm there. I'm a programmer and I'm permitted to override the main computer for emergency situations, making it possible to move *Folion* in case something happens that it wasn't programmed to respond to. As an example, I ordered Clara to move when

87

that freighter didn't slow as it came at us because she's not programmed for that kind of situation but it happened too fast for us to totally get out of the way. If it had been a meteor she would have automatically moved to avoid the hit. No one foresaw a drunken captain not reducing his speed, and since Clara had already given him clearance to dock, her automated collision alarm wasn't triggered as it approached. Normally when the alarm is activated it would have her start the engines to avoid it."

"Clara?"

"She is the main computer that runs and oversees the ship and the bots. She's got artificial intelligence and can learn from interaction with the clients just as the bots do but after a few problems arose with the bots, they knew someone needed to monitor what they were learning. Clara couldn't do that."

"What kind of problems?" He shifted his weight and his body seemed to relax.

A grin curved Megan's lips. "Well, as an example, one of the clients happened to be into a little rough sex."

"And you find this amusing?" His eyebrow arched.

"He taught one of the bots to spank him and told her what a turn-on that was so when the next client came, she grabbed him, bent him over the bed, and spanked his ass. She thought that would arouse him." A laugh escaped her. "He wasn't amused. He became really angry about the whole experience and wanted the company to pay for the bruising he suffered from her smacks. Now I have to go over what they've learned from clients and delete some of it so that doesn't happen again."

A muscle in his jaw jumped. "You have reviewed everything my men and I have done with your bots?"

"No." She shook her head. "Not exactly. The bots are programmed to ask questions if a client does something outside of their programming parameters and I answer their questions. Now they would question if it were acceptable to spank a client. I tell them no and they delete that information."

"Have you ever had to review anything I've done?"

She shifted her weight on the bed, fidgeted, and her gaze lowered to his chest. "Um..." Heat flushed her cheeks.

"What did you review?" His voice deepened.

She glanced up at him, seeing his tense expression, and she found his black boots suddenly very interesting. "It was just once and you didn't teach her anything I had to have her erase from her programming."

"What did I do?" He took a step closer.

Wow, is it hot in here? No, it's just me, she thought. She forced herself to meet his gaze and just open her mouth. "You have a preference that the bots weren't programmed for."

"What did I do?"

"You examined her vaginal area very closely when you had her pose with her lower region exposed to your view. Clients don't do that normally. It had her questioning if she should use that with other clients to turn them on or if it should be deleted."

Megan could have sworn the man blushed as he glanced away, the color in his cheeks darkened just slightly. He moved slowly to his bed and he sat down on the edge of it hard, making it creak under his heavy weight, just a few feet from her. He didn't look at her.

"I'm curious by nature."

"No need to explain. I find them fascinating myself." She shrugged when he met her gaze again. "I've had to repair a few of them. They are very lifelike."

"You're a programmer and you do hardware repairs as well?"

"Minor ones. We have a maintenance bot onboard *Folion* that does it but she goes offline for upgrades from time to time so I handle repairing units for that day when it happens. I've actually only had to repair two of them. They don't get damaged often."

"What happened to them?"

"One had skin damage from a client who scratched her and the other one a breast problem when one of the gel packs under her artificial skin ruptured. I had to replace it."

Ice smiled. "That's what is under there?"

She nodded. "They feel pretty close to the real thing." A grin split her lips again. "I never thought I'd have to grope breasts but I had to so I could get them just right. They have to be perfectly aligned with each other." She paused. "There I was, hand on each breast, squeezing to make sure they felt and looked the same. I had to adjust the gel a few times."

"You must enjoy your job." He still grinned, looking really handsome.

"If I were into girls, hell yes, but I'm not. I'm kind of uncomfortable with that aspect of my job, actually. I had her shut down because it was just too weird having her blinking at me and asking me questions while I messed with her girls."

A deep, wonderful chuckle poured from Ice's mouth. His eyes lit up with amusement as he stared at her. He got the slightest little laugh lines on his temples. It amazed her and before she gave it a thought, she leaned over, inches from him, and her hand reached for his face. His eyes widened with shock and he stopped laughing as his hand shot out, wrapping around her wrist to halt her from touching him.

"What are you doing?"

She backed away immediately. "I'm sorry."

He stood quickly, frowning down at her, still gripping her. "What were you doing? Answer me."

"You get laugh lines. This is the first time I've ever seen you really laugh."

"That surprises you?" His voice deepened.

"A little, yeah. I don't know much about cyborgs but I thought you'd have a lot in common with the bots. They have certain limitations on their expressions and I assumed you would too."

"I'm made of flesh and blood."

"Oh. I wasn't sure if you had real skin. I thought you might have synthetic because of the color of it. It feels the same as mine does but they've come so far with technology." She glanced at his hand gripping her

91

wrist, studying the gray color. "Do you know why they didn't make you human-flesh toned?" She looked up at him.

"They didn't want us to be mistaken for human." He paused and then slowly sat back down. His fingers unwrapped from her wrist as he locked gazes with her. "Proceed. You may touch me."

Now that she thought about what to do, she hesitated before lifting her hand. She barely brushed her fingertips along his cheekbone. His skin was soft, smooth, and warm, just the way she remembered from exploring him while he slept. Now he was aware of her touching him and she told him what she thought.

"You're so warm, more so than I am."

"I'm not a bot." He took a deep breath. "Cyborgs were cloned and genes were altered. All hereditary diseases were filtered out, only the strongest genes were used, and they added in some artificial ones to help us heal faster and live longer. I have implants and stronger bones than you do. I also run slightly higher in temperature but only by a few degrees."

"I noticed that you have tattoos but they are so faint they are barely noticeable unless I'm up close. I've never seen anything similar to them. Do they have meaning?"

He hesitated. "It's the cyborg language we created. All cyborgs have them but I didn't like the idea of being branded. It's our way of identifying each other so it was necessary to have it done. I just had them put my information on one arm and in smaller writing so it wasn't as irritating to me."

"Oh." Megan nodded. "What do they say?"

"My name and what I do. When we first started to build our city on our new home world, the work was very harsh. Some of our people died and since there were many of us, it was hard to keep track of names. It's why they decided to brand us this way. They could identify those who were injured or dead."

Her gaze flickered down his leather-clad body. "What kind of implants do you have?"

He tilted his head, moving away from her touch so she let her hand drop, then he straightened his head again. "There are some inside my head to help me communicate with technology. Emotions were not expected when we were created so they installed chips to shut off sections of our brains in an attempt to block them. I also have a heart monitor in my chest so, in case of failure, it will shock it back into functioning."

Her gaze flicked down to his broad chest and then back up again. "Why the backup system? Do cyborgs have weak hearts?"

"I'm designated to be a mechanic and work with electronics. If a strong current is ever introduced into my body during an accident, it could stop my heart."

"Hence the backup system," she guessed aloud. "Well, I guess that's handy."

"Yes."

"So your emotions are blocked? That's weird. I figured you had them since you have a need for..." Her voice trailed off and her mouth slammed closed.

His eyebrow lifted. "Sex?"

She gave a sharp nod. "Yes. The bots don't have a sex drive. They just do what they are programmed for. They recharge when they aren't in use and just stay at their docking stations inside the rooms. They couldn't care less if they are activated or if they stay dormant for months."

He stared into her eyes. "I have a very active sex drive but I do have the ability to shut it down if I wish. I don't. I enjoy having access to everything that I am."

"Oh. I would too."

"You have had sex with me and you still believed me to be more bot than humanoid?"

She hesitated. "You taste really sweet."

Astonishment widened his stare. "Sweet?"

Megan knew her cheeks were warming from the blush spreading there. "When you come, it tastes sweet, which made me think that perhaps they made you flavored that way and that got me to thinking that maybe you were more artificial than not."

An uncomfortable silence stretched as they watched each other. She'd obviously been a little too blunt and had stunned the cyborg speechless. Megan started when a loud buzz sounded in the room. Ice stood.

"It's the food Blackie ordered."

Megan didn't recognize the cyborg who brought her meal. She wondered how many of them were on the ship in all but didn't ask. Ice nodded at the other man and accepted the tray. The male at the door hesitated.

"Why feed her?"

"Silence," Ice ordered him.

The man looked down at the tray of food, paled, and then nodded. "I see."

The man glanced at Megan, a look of pity on his features, and then spun on his heel to walk away. The door closed and Ice faced her with tray in hand.

"Here is your meal." He hesitated, looking uncertain, and took a step back, the movement opposite of his words. It was almost as if he didn't want to feed her.

No one had ever accused Megan of being dimwitted. *Why feed her?* That cyborg had given her a look that reflected pity. She studied Ice and saw his grim expression.

"You are supposed to eat this." Anger clearly sounded in his tone.

She wiggled back on the mattress until she ended up in the corner of the bed with her body pressed tightly to both walls. Panic welled inside her. "I'm not hungry," she lied.

He looked away from her, stared instead at the floor for long seconds, and then his gaze lifted. Regret was an easy expression to read on his handsome face.

"Oh God." Tears welled in her eyes as she stared into his beautiful ones. "I swore I wouldn't tell anyone about you. I could have done that months ago but I didn't. All I would have had to do was open up a communication with Earth to turn you in. I know you aren't sure if you can trust me but if I'd tried to collect a reward for you, they would have been

95

waiting to attack you the second you docked with *Folion* or even before you reached it."

He watched her silently, holding the tray, his expression carefully cleared of emotion now.

"Please believe me. I'm no threat to you or your other cyborg people, Ice. I'd never hurt you in any way."

"I tend to believe you. I gave you an opportunity to harm me yet you didn't do it."

The tray in his hands said otherwise. She could feel it in her gut, and also knew something had been done to the food. She stared into his shuttered gaze again, seeing the remote look.

"Is it poisoned?"

His mouth tensed, the only reaction he allowed to show. "No."

"You're lying."

The big cyborg took a deep breath before he expelled it slowly. "It's not poisoned but it is drugged with a strong sedative that will put you to sleep."

"Why?" It hurt that he'd be a part of anything that would harm her. They'd shared so much in the time they'd spent together. Disbelief and shock tore at her. "Ice? Are you going to hurt me?" She fought back tears.

He looked away and then met her gaze. "I don't want to cause you any harm." His jaw clenched. "Believe that if nothing else."

Megan watched as he seemed to struggle with whatever thoughts he had and then his face cleared of emotion.

"You are aware of us. We have a council and they have deemed it too risky to allow you to return to Earth with the knowledge you possess. We are close to our home world and your Earth Government may realize that if you were to talk to them. They could start searching this area, hunting for our planet and they would find it. While we have a defense system, we don't want to test it. We enjoy the freedom to travel and do not want a war with Earth. We left your planet to avoid just that."

"I'd never tell the government about you. I don't know much about cyborgs but I heard every word you said about getting a real raw deal in the past when they made you and then tried to wipe you out." She paused. "I'm not a fan of mass murder."

"The council has determined that you are too much of a risk. They believe you are either a spy for Earth Government or that you are a bounty hunter searching for a large group of cyborgs to collect a reward."

"That's not true. I'm just a programmer who got offered a lot of money to live out in deep space on the *Folion* and my existence was deemed classified so some jackasses didn't try to find me to attempt to use me to get control of Clara so they could steal it."

He studied her. "I tend to believe you, if that matters, but orders have to be followed. It's not my call to make."

"So you're going to drug me and then what?" Megan feared asking and suspected the answer already. The idea that he'd do that to her had her fighting tears again. She had believed she could trust him to never hurt her but she'd been wrong, obviously. "Are you going to kill me?" Her voice broke.

Ice physically flinched. He took another slow, long breath. "It's a method Earth Government trained cyborgs to use to take a life painlessly while the target slept but I can't do it." He suddenly spun, slamming the tray against the table. "I don't want you to die but an order has been issued. I can't disobey a direct order from the council but I find myself unable to comply either. We're both in a hell of a lot of trouble, Megan."

Chapter Six

The reality of Megan's situation stunned, horrified, and kept her mute while she stared at Ice. The cyborg council wanted her dead, she had been deemed a threat to his people, and Ice had been given orders to kill her.

"Blackie lied to me about setting me free."

"He did. It was his version of kindness to lure you into a sense of false security that your life had been spared so I could say goodbye to you without your tears or pleading for your life."

"What an asshole. I mean, I guess for him it would be considered almost sweet but I don't appreciate it." She had to fight to think through the panic.

"Agreed. If it were up to me I would prefer to believe you and drop you off with the bots on Hixton Station just the way we originally planned but it is not in my authority to give you that. The safety of my people is at stake and the risk is too great to allow you to go free."

"I don't want to die," she whispered.

"I can't kill you." He paused. "Blackie will most likely come here since I'm unable to do it. You will not die at my hands."

She stared at him, fighting tears, and managed to hold them at bay. "Is that supposed to comfort me?"

"Yes."

"It doesn't."

"I apologize. I can only stall for time before he comes to make certain the council's orders were followed."

"May I talk to this council? Maybe I can change their minds."

"The decision has been made and nothing you could say would affect them. We have to follow orders or my ship will be in violation of the council." He sighed. "We would both die then."

Her brain struggled to take it all in but underneath the panic, she wondered at Ice's inability to kill her. She had to know. "So why can't you kill me yourself? Why not just shoot me or something? You're strong enough to kill me in a hundred ways I can think up with your bare hands alone."

He hesitated. "You fascinate me and I find myself feeling strangely protective of you. I am unable to carry out their order. They will be very displeased with me."

"Thanks." She wondered if he could pick up on sarcasm. When he frowned at her, she assumed that he could. "If this is how cyborgs are—they can just order women to be murdered—I can see why Earth Government wanted them dead. Apparently, most of you are heartless bastards."

He nodded. "We were made this way by them."

"Don't your leaders know the difference between right and wrong? Doesn't this council have any compassion? Doesn't it bother them just a tiny bit to kill an unarmed woman?"

"I do not know. I can only speak for myself, Megan."

"But you're going to allow someone on this ship to kill me?"

"I have no choice but I won't allow anyone to cause you pain when they follow the order."

"Don't you see something seriously wrong with that?"

"Yes."

"Then don't do it. Just drop me off with the bots."

"I have to follow orders even if I do not agree with them. They are the Cyborg Council and it is my duty to do as they demand even if I find it highly distasteful. I really don't want you to die, Megan. I am attempting to think of a solution where you can be freed but I am coming up with nothing so far."

She watched him while he stared back at her. In a lot of ways he was similar to the bots if he was compelled to follow orders and would be destroyed if he wouldn't do as he was told—if he'd told her the truth about them killing him if he disobeyed a direct order. The programmer inside her understood the complexities of machines and how they kept within their guidelines. She swallowed the lump that formed in her throat.

"What are your orders exactly?"

"To kill you."

"Today?"

"An exact time wasn't specified but it's implied that the order be followed quickly. It is our way. Cyborgs aren't known for procrastinating. The council deemed it too dangerous to allow you the opportunity to contact Earth Government."

It might be something she could work with, a flaw in their programming, as it were. She hesitated. "What if I were to stay on this ship?"

His eyebrows arched. "And what would be the point of that? You can't stay in my quarters indefinitely."

She hesitated. "Why not? I can't contact anyone if I'm locked in your room, correct? That's logical. If I'm no threat then there's no reason to kill me."

He said nothing.

Her gaze drifted around the small room. It would be cramped with the two of them sharing it. Her gaze landed and held on the handsome cyborg in front of her. She'd had plenty of fantasies about him and figured she could find lots of ways to keep amused if she were living with Ice. Life could be worse and he sure beat death.

She got to her feet. "You visited *Folion* five times in the past three months that I'm aware of."

He frowned. "What does this have to do with stating your plan to stay on the ship to avoid the council's sentencing?"

Would he go for it? She'd never been an overly forward type of woman. As a matter of fact, she enjoyed it when men pursued her, until she'd seen Ice. He'd had her tossing her old-fashioned thinking but she wanted him, had for a long time, and he could keep her alive if he'd agree to allow her to stay in his room.

"You like sex and you seemed to enjoy it with me the few times we've been together."

He said nothing but his eyes narrowed.

"If you allow me to share your room with you then you get sex any time you want it." She paused. "I know your quarters are small but we could have a hell of a lot of fun sharing your bed."

His reaction was swift and unexpected. He growled low in his throat. "No. I will think of something else."

"No?" Megan gaped at him, stunned. "Did you hear what I said? Free sex, as much of it as you can handle, and all you have to do is allow me stay here so you don't have to kill me. You said you didn't want that to happen to me so here's a loophole for us both."

"No," he repeated. He paused. "I will not allow them to kill you if I can help it."

She admitted it really stung that he'd said no as pain burned a little inside her chest. The guy she'd gone to great lengths to have sex with, the cyborg she'd spent months having sexual fantasies about, had just rejected her outright over the concept of having a longer relationship with her.

"The sex is good between us, Ice." *It is for me anyway*, she thought, hoping he could say the same. If it hadn't been, he was a world-class actor because it had sure sounded as though he enjoyed being inside her. "Why don't you want me now?"

He backed up more and leaned against the wall next to the door. "It was one thing to spend a short period of time with you but you're asking for a lot more than that. I prefer bots to real females. As much as I would wish to spare your life, it wouldn't work between us. I'll come up with another way to protect you."

Her eyebrow arched in disbelief. "I thought you only visited *Folion* to use them because they weren't a risk to telling anyone you existed."

"Bots do as they are told, there is no emotional connection, and they don't expect things from me. Humans and cyborgs are not a good match."

"Why not?" Curiosity had her asking. She'd seen him have sex plenty of times, had sex with him, and he didn't do anything a human guy didn't. He'd never damaged a bot and hadn't done her any harm. She wasn't about to mention any of that to him but maybe he didn't know those things. "You are bigger than me but you're not going to break me unless you've really been restraining yourself every time you've touched me or a bot."

"How would you know if I'd ever damaged a bot?"

"I told you that I'm the programmer, and though I rarely do hardware repairs, I read the reports. You've never so much as scratched one of them."

She hoped that was a good enough answer because she sure wasn't admitting her voyeurism concerning his sex life on *Folion*. He'd get pissed off over that violation.

"My concern is not damaging you." He pushed away from the wall. "You don't understand my dilemma." His expression showed emotion...anguish.

"Tell me what you have against having sex with me."

A frown marred his lips. "We discovered a ship of ours that had been thought lost forever and with it, a large group of cyborgs who had survived."

"Okay. And that means what exactly?"

He took a deep breath. "My coloring is unique."

She stared at him. "I can see that. You have those beautiful eyes and your hair is just striking. I've never seen someone with streaks like yours without them putting them there. I assume it's natural to you?"

He nodded. "I'll make this simple so you can understand."

Megan arched her eyebrow at him. "Okay. You know I'm a programmer though and not a nitwit, right?"

"I am not questioning your intelligence, Megan. Cyborg laws are complicated. When we escaped Earth, we stole ships to flee to safety and one of them contained the majority of our females. Their ship was lost. When we settled on our new home world the council's first priority became instilling laws that made sure that the much larger population of males had equal opportunity to the limited supply of females."

"You make it sound as though women are objects."

He frowned at her. "Their number-one objective became setting up family units and making sure we had a future as we began to build Cyborg City. That meant that our females had to form family units with multiple males. Every cyborg was given the responsibility of having a child each to make certain our race continued to thrive and grow. Two children were preferable but having at least one per adult is mandatory."

Children? Megan gulped. She didn't want any of those. Her life wasn't stable enough, she had never stayed in one place for long, and it wouldn't be right to drag a child around in her nomad way of life. She knew from firsthand experience how messed up they could be. Her father had been a traveling salesman, home had been a space shuttle, and she'd grown up really lonely.

People didn't stay, everyone left her, and she'd learned to never get too attached to people after having her heart broken time and time again when she'd allowed herself to care for someone. Her mother had abandoned both her husband and her child and her father had ditched her the day she'd been old enough to fend for herself since he considered her a nuisance. She'd sworn off any future that involved marriage or kids.

Ice continued. "Most male cyborgs were created sterile but we found a way around that with drugs that reverse the process temporarily but it isn't effective for all males. With that factor added into the numbers, breeding pacts with a dozen males in each one was implemented."

"What is a breeding pact?"

"Will you let me finish without interrupting?"

"Sorry. Go ahead."

He took a deep breath, blowing out air. "It meant that if a male wasn't able to impregnate the female in his family unit to have that one mandated child, he could call upon one of the other males in his breeding pact who had viable sperm to donate it." He paused. "Before you ask, artificial insemination proved highly ineffective so the males actually have intercourse with the female to get her pregnant. It is less stressful on her that way and more enjoyable."

Megan had no words, too shocked to speak. Ice didn't have that problem. He watched her closely though, his eyes narrowed.

106

"I avoided joining a family unit because I need to be in control of my own life as much as possible. Cyborg females tend to be very aggressive because of their value—they are aware of it. They are…" He paused. "Assertive with males."

She understood. "They rule the roost."

"I don't understand that wording."

"They tell you what to do and you have to do it."

His features tightened into a grimace. "Yes. If a male joins a family unit and he doesn't make that female happy, she can file charges with the council and have that male deemed unsuitable. No other female will touch a male with that on his record. I probably would have been dismissed from all breeding pacts which tempted me because I found it difficult to donate so many times but I didn't want all my options to be forever closed in case I ever did want to form a family unit sometime in the distant future."

"You had to go to bed with a lot of women?" She wondered how many cyborg women he'd slept with but didn't ask.

"I'm considered a rarity with my hair, eye color, and strength. I was called upon many times by males in my pact to donate when their females requested my DNA."

That's a big yes, she thought. Not that she could blame cyborg women for wanting Ice in their beds. If someone wanted kids, he'd make some really cute babies.

"I bet that was tough, having to sleep with a lot of women." She held back her snort. He was male after all and what guy would complain about having to nail a lot of women? "Poor you."

He crossed the distance between them in seconds, grabbed her and jerked her to her feet while anger clearly twisted his features as he glared down at her.

"It wasn't the sex I minded but do you know how many times those donations took? Twenty-eight times the results were successful." He took a ragged breath. "Twenty-eight viable children who were born healthy, mostly male, and I am not permitted to see them, talk to them, or ever be a part of their lives." He took another harsh breath. "I told myself the same thing all males do when called upon. It is just a donation and I did my duty for the good of our future, but then…"

He went silent, shoving Megan onto her ass on the bed, and spun away. He put distance between them, running his fingers through his hair. He stood there.

Megan regretted her words. "Then what?" She spoke softly since she'd seen pain in his beautiful eyes before he'd turned away from her. "Talk to me, Ice."

When he spoke, his voice softened, nearly a whisper. "I was off duty for a week on Garden, my home world, and I needed to do some shopping. I saw a woman I recognized in the store. I had been bred to her a year before and in her arms she held…my son." He turned to stare at Megan, his eyes suspiciously wet looking before he blinked rapidly to dissipate the tears. "I'm certain of my assessment of him being my son since he shared my rare coloring and he smiled at me."

Her heart wrenched for the raw pain she couldn't miss in Ice's features.

"He is my son, my blood, and yet I am not permitted to speak to him, to touch him, or to claim him in any way. Twenty-eight children are on Garden and they are mine but I have no rights to them. Can you imagine in your human mind how that feels or how difficult it would be to have that reality slam into you? It did me. It wasn't just sperm donations anymore for duty. Pieces of my soul were being given to couples and I would never know my own offspring."

She pushed off the bed, stood, and inched toward him. "I'm so sorry." Tears filled her eyes. She hated to see him hurting that badly, to see how deeply it affected him.

He looked away, his gaze going to the floor. "That ship with most of our women was recovered recently. They'd bred mostly female children while they were lost and they were recently returned to Garden. The council took the new numbers into account and changed the laws. Now their first priority since women aren't such a shortage is to watch the DNA matching of the children born so that our males aren't overused in breeding. They removed all males who have had over twenty successful donations from breeding pacts so future generations don't face a higher percentage of unsuitable breeding choices with DNA conflicts from the male donors used for their conceptions."

"So they can't make you have more children."

He spun away, his back to her again, and suddenly punched the wall hard. It stunned Megan as she watched him shake his fist a little and then it fell to dangle at his side. He'd left a mark on the bulkhead wall from his

109

fist and a small sound drew her attention to the floor. Drops of red blood started to stain it.

"You hurt yourself."

She reached for his arm, moving closer, but when her fingers touched his wrist he jerked away, putting distance between them again. He stopped by the door, keeping his back to her and just bled on the floor.

"I was called upon by a breeding-pact member when we first arrived at Garden on our last trip there a few weeks ago. The council decided to change the law two days after the mandatory donation." He snarled the words and then spun back around. "Do you know what I read in the same order that stated you were to die?" He glared at her. "They gave me notification that my donation was successful. Another child will be born, mine, and they changed the law two days too late to prevent me from creating yet another life I will have no right to know. Why couldn't they have done that when we first arrived with those women and children? Why did the damn council wait those days?"

"I'm so sorry, Ice." She hurt for him, hated to see him suffering, and realized how much that had to mess with his mind.

"I'm finally free from ever being called upon to breed by force but they activated my sperm for that last donation." He continued to glare at her. "Every time I touch you I am risking a pregnancy with you, Megan. I knew I could pull out of you for a few days but I can't do that long term. I could only locate one medicondom aboard this shuttle and I used it that first time with you. I have no access to more until we can visit an Earth-based station for supplies. Cyborg pre-cum isn't effective so the risk is in my not removing myself from inside your body before I release active sperm. That is difficult to do for me because the pleasure is too great between us at times and I nearly lost my control. I could impregnate you while my sperm is still active for the next two months."

"Ice—"

He cut her off. "It could happen and I'm not willing to take those chances. They have ordered your death and I can't see a way of saving you long term. I refuse to lose another child to the council and their orders. They won't care if you're pregnant when they kill you because my DNA is considered overused so there's no value in any child I might produce." His voice turned so harsh, he snarled his words. "They informed me that because of how successful the breeding pact was, I am no longer mandated to produce a child of my own. I have lost too much of my soul already and I am getting too attached to you. I just can't take the pain I could possibly face and will have to endure because I've run the odds in my mind. That's the truth, Megan. It's better to lose you now than suffer a greater loss of both of you."

Something inside Megan broke for him, pretty sure it was her heart. All doubts about his ability to feel were gone. She walked to him and ignored how his body stiffened at her approach. She reached out and took his injured hand, still fisted at his side, her fingers curling around it.

"You can't get me pregnant. I come from a messed up childhood so I didn't want to ever have kids. I got implanted with birth control before I ever started having sex. Unless it's removed there's no risk involved."

Megan hoped that would comfort him but instead he shook his head. "I can't do this even though that's half the problem solved. I attacked another cyborg today, protecting you. He is going to have to report me to the council for my actions and it made me realize how attached I have gotten to you." The hand she gripped moved and his fingers curled with hers, holding onto her. "I'm finally free to be my own man. First they controlled me when we were under Earth Government's command and then the council forced me to give more of myself than I wanted to. You threaten all of that."

"How?"

Their gazes locked together. His thumb rubbed the side of her pinky. "I finally have control of my life, my body, and you're asking something of me that I'm not willing to risk."

He was a control freak. She'd realized that right off the bat with Ice. It wasn't just a preference of his, it had become his way of protecting himself against more pain. She could understand that after having everyone in her own life let her down. It had really messed her up when her parents had abandoned her one at a time. Ice didn't want to allow himself to feel too much and then lose her. Again, something she could understand.

She released his hand and took a few steps back, never looking away from him. "You preferred the bots because you couldn't get attached to them."

He sighed. "Yes."

"And you don't want to get more emotionally involved with me." It stung but she knew he did it to guard his heart.

112

"Yes. I don't want you to die either."

He was torn. Megan was falling in love with the cyborg even more for having emotions she could relate to and understand. He happened to be more perfect for her than she'd ever guessed or hoped because he had flaws and emotional damage just the way she did. She no longer had any doubt about that whatsoever as she studied his beautiful silvery-blue eyes and the haunted look in them that he tried to hide from her.

"You won't get attached to a bot and I don't want to die." She backed up more, straightened her shoulders, and masked her features. "I'll be your bot. How may I serve you?"

Ice's features showed his shock as it sunk in what she said and what it meant. His mouth parted and then he frowned. "Megan…"

"I don't want to die. You don't want to get attached." She lifted her chin. "It's the perfect way for both of us to live. How may I serve you?"

"You're not a bot."

"I could be one. If anyone knows them, it's me. I program the damn things. This solves both of our problems. I get to stay with you and you get all the sex you want without the risk of getting to know me."

They watched each other for long moments. Ice turned away, used the cleansing unit to wash his injured hand, and then dried it. When he turned, all emotions were hidden on his features and his gaze grew chilly.

"Bots follow orders without argument or question. That is how I need my females to be."

She hesitated, knowing she'd offered to do this. "I can do that." It wouldn't be easy, she wasn't real good at following orders to the letter, but this was sex they were talking about. She had a submissive streak in the bedroom. "I really can do this, Ice."

His beautiful blue gaze ran down her body quickly and then jerked back up. "A test then?"

"A test of what?"

"A test to see if you can follow orders. If you can act as though you are a bot and swear to not get emotional, I will allow you to stay in my room."

"And you won't kill me?"

"I already can't bring myself to kill you, Megan. Your plan of action is logical. You're no threat to my home world if you are locked in a room where you have no access to communications. I want to be honest. I highly doubt the council will reverse their decision no matter how long you stay here so don't get your hopes up of that happening. The available sex is tempting but I will be in total control if we do this." Something softened in his gaze. "I just can't risk it otherwise."

Getting his heart broken, she thought, understanding. She pushed back her nervousness and nodded. She could do submissive. She'd had a boyfriend once who was heavily into that shit. It had been a little hot until she found out he liked that in all aspects of his life. She could be submissive in the bedroom but outside of it, she made her own choices.

She attempted not to be anxious as she closed the distance between them. She stopped inches in front of him, so close she could touch him by just lifting her hands. Her chin tipped back so she could stare up at the much-taller man. He was so very handsome with his strong masculine features and those amazing light-blue eyes with the silver streaks.

"How may I serve you?"

"We'll try this plan of yours." He hesitated. "Strip now." His voice deepened.

I can totally be submissive, she thought. She turned away from him and started to strip out of her borrowed clothing. When naked, she turned to face him again, stunned to see that he'd removed his own clothing very quickly. She hadn't heard a thing to indicate he'd undressed. She'd have to remember how stealthy he could be.

"You do as I say or this isn't going to work. Am I clear?"

"Crystal."

He studied her and she saw something in his expression that made her tense. She had seen that look before with a few of her employers when they were pissed off and about to push her into quitting. This was one job that she wasn't about to easily let go. She watched him without saying a word as he went to the built-in drawers, bent to show his nice, firm, rounded ass, and opened the lowest one. In seconds he turned and she stared at what he had in his hand.

"Come here."

Shit! She froze in fear at seeing the ropelike, long belt he held fisted in his hand. He watched her very closely.

"I said come here."

Her gaze locked with his. "You're scaring me a little. I know you got a little worked up over our conversation but you know I'm not responsible for the bad things done to you, right?"

"I won't hurt you, Megan. There are things I wished to experience with the bots but they aren't as mobile as you are."

"Can you tell me what you want to do?"

"You're not behaving as a bot." He frowned. "I'm willing to do anything to protect you, even live with you if you understand we can't get attached to each other, but for it to be a successful partnership you need to go along with the plan we have set forth."

"Plan? You mean act as if I'm a bot so it's easier for you to pretend I'm not real?"

He frowned at her. "It is to remind you as well that this is a partnership and not a relationship."

"You're not treating me as if I'm a bot—in my defense."

His lips curved and amusement lit his blue eyes. "How would you know?"

Double shit! I have to watch what I say or he's going to figure out I watched him do them. "You never damaged them."

"I have no intention of harming you in any way." He approached her instead of having her come to him. "I couldn't stand to watch you hit, so use logic."

"You won't hurt me?"

"I won't hurt you," he confirmed softly. "Put your hands together in front of you, wrists together as if you were going to pray to your God."

Hesitation was instant but then she did as he demanded. She lifted her arms and entwined her fingers together, locking her palms at face level. Ice started to wrap the soft material around her wrists, securing them together firmly but not tight enough to cut off circulation to her hands. She had to admit to feeling strong curiosity but no longer any fear. He tied it off and then stepped back, tugging on her to follow him. She was leashed by the long trailing end that he held in his hand.

He led her to the cleansing unit and stepped inside, leading her into the small space with him. She wondered what they were doing in there unless he had a sudden urge to get clean but he didn't activate the wall to start the foam. Instead he maneuvered until her back pressed against the wall with her facing him. He reached up and she lifted her chin to watch as he threw the ropelike belt over a hook near the ceiling. He had to lean against her and go up on tiptoe to reach it to make that toss but he did it. Her heart pounded, having no clue what he'd do or what he had planned.

He lowered to stand in front of her and held the belt with one raised hand. Their gazes locked and she suddenly gasped as he lowered that arm, his biceps straining as he used his strength to pull down on it while it lifted her body from the floor. His other hand slipped around her waist, taking most of her weight off her wrists.

"What—"

"Quiet," he ordered in a rough voice. "Reach up and grab the bar above you."

She dangled inches from the floor, her arms above her head, the belt being used as a pulley system from the hook above. She bit her lip, staring at him, and then gasped as he lowered his arm more, wrapping the belt around his wrist, twist after twist, inching her higher from the floor.

Megan had guessed that cyborgs were strong but he literally held all of her weight with his left arm and the one around her waist. She suddenly knew how a puppet felt as he pulled her higher. He didn't stop until her breasts were level with his mouth. He stared at them and then leaned in, his mouth closing over one. She fumbled for the bar, her fingers frantically grabbed hold, clenching it.

"Oh God," she moaned.

Ice's mouth wasn't gentle. It was hot, wet, and he sucked on her nipple hard. The sensation that rippled through her brought sheer pleasure. His arm slid away from her waist and his now-free hand gripped her thigh, caressing upward until his thumb pressed against her pussy.

He shifted his hand and then his fingers cupped her mound, holding her there firmly as his teeth nipped her in a shocking jolt of something akin to pain but it didn't exactly hurt. It was erotic as hell and her body responded full force. She realized how wet she'd grown when his fingers slid between her sex lips and he played with the slippery moisture that came from her. He groaned against her breast and released it, going for the other one.

"Ice," she moaned.

He didn't respond verbally but two of his fingers suddenly drove up inside her pussy as his mouth sucked harder on her nipple. Pleasure seared through her and the cool wall behind her made her even more aware of how much warmth his skin radiated where it pressed against her stomach as he leaned in more, finger-fucking her harder and faster. His mouth played hell on her nipple.

"Yes," she moaned.

Ice suddenly froze, his fingers slowly withdrew from her pussy and his mouth left her breast. Megan opened her eyes to stare into his gorgeous ones below her since he'd lifted her above his head. He lowered her slightly and she let her gaze follow his to his erect cock until he had her dangling hip to hip with him. They stared at each other.

"I can do anything to you. Does that turn you on? You're so wet."

She cleared her throat. "Yes," she admitted honestly. "You're so strong too and that really makes me hotter."

"I admit that your delicateness makes me hurt with need. You're so unlike cyborg women. I really find you fascinating and no woman has ever made me long to possess her the way I do you."

His free arm slid between her thighs, lifting one of them up over his forearm, and his body moved closer so her knee bent against his rib cage. He adjusted his hips and pressed his cock right against her vaginal entrance, never looking away from her gaze once.

"If there is sheer pleasure, you are it, Megan." He slowly pressed forward, entering her.

Megan closed her eyes in pure ecstasy as he stretched her, filled her with that hard, thick length of his cock. She forced them open though and stared back into his heated gaze. "You're a dangerous man, Ice. You make me feel too much, since we're being so honest."

He sank in deeper, lowering her weight just slightly as his leg brushed her other one aside to drape over his thigh. It spread her legs wider open to his hips and cock. He buried his cock totally inside her body. She could

119

feel his full length sheathed inside her. The heavenly sensation had her moaning louder.

"I'm going to fuck you, baby." He paused, tilting his head just slightly. "And then I'm going to do the one thing I've wanted to most since I first touched you."

"What?" Her voice shook a little and she had no idea what he thought or wanted.

"I'm going to come inside you and fill you with my mark. You're my bot, Megan, and I'm going to keep you for a while."

"I can live with that." She lifted her chin. "Will you kiss me?"

"I'm going to do everything to you." He lowered his mouth, taking possession of hers.

Chapter Seven

Cyborgs should have been banned on Earth just for the sinful way they could kiss. Megan moaned and tried to not bite Ice as he proceeded to fuck her hard and deep. She hung there helpless, pinned against the cold cleansing-unit wall, and could only feel pure ecstasy on so many levels that it overwhelmed her. He held most of her weight so the it didn't hurt her hands or wrists.

Hanging by her arms made her more aware of so many things like how his body rubbed against hers with every upward drive of his hips hammering her and, being unable to move, she could just feel. He tore his mouth from hers and went for her throat. His teeth raked the side of her neck and then bit down. He didn't bite her hard enough to hurt but it sent shock waves throughout her system with the firm, erotic grip he kept. He moaned with her as he slowed the pace and released her neck.

"Wrap your legs around me."

He helped her, shifting her leg until she locked her ankles behind his spine. His beefy ass helped keep her heels from sliding down his body. His arm hooked under her ass as his other arm lifted her a few inches higher until they were perfectly aligned. He drove into her faster again but tilted her hips just enough that her clit rubbed against him.

"Oh God, Ice," she moaned, letting her face rest on his broad shoulder. She fought the urge to bite him back.

She came hard, the climax tearing through her body, and her teeth sank into his skin. He jerked against her, his body tensing, and then a loud groan tore from his lips as he pressed her tighter to the wall, nearly crushing her there, and she could feel him inside her as he came. Heat spread inside her vagina and she shivered at the extra sensation of pleasure. He backed off enough for her to gasp in air now that she wasn't compressed to the wall. She released him from her teeth and stared at the bite mark on his light-gray skin.

"I'm sorry," she panted.

"I'm not." His voice deepened into a rumble next to her ear as he nuzzled her with the side of his face. His breath tickled her neck as he turned his head and their gazes locked.

"I bit you."

"It made me come harder."

"You like a little pain with your pleasure, huh?"

He flashed a grin. "I guess that I do. I never knew that about myself before but if that was an indication, then yes."

"Too bad you had me tied up then because I have a feeling I would have clawed you with my nails because of how good you feel inside me then."

His arm adjusted from under her ass to around her waist, anchoring her securely against his body as the little bit of tension on her wrists suddenly abated. She glanced away from him to watch him unwind the belt from his wrist. She saw dark marks there from it but then got distracted as her arms lowered and blood flowed back to her limbs. Her wrists were still bound together so she just slipped her arms over his head, holding him as she met his gaze again. He had the most beautiful eyes she'd ever seen.

"I didn't hurt you, did I?"

She shook her head, not looking away from him. "No. I enjoyed the hell out of that but I do love, to touch you."

"You will get to do that often since we now share living space. I promised you food and I need to go get it if you wish to eat." He paused. "Let me go. I'll put you down and untie you. We'll cleanse together."

She hated to release him but grudgingly lifted her arms as he slid her down his body when she unlocked her legs from his hips. Her feet touched the floor and he stepped back, releasing her waist. In seconds, he freed her wrists. She saw the marks but she doubted it would bruise since the material was soft and thick enough to have supported her weight. She glanced at his wrist, seeing the marks from where he'd held her weight already disappearing.

"Close your eyes," he warned as he reached behind them to toss away the belt and hit the button to raise the wall that enclosed them totally in the tight space of the cleansing unit.

She barely did it before he hit the button and foam sprayed them both. He moved back a little so it went between them. She shivered when the foam melted on her oversensitive flesh, tickling her skin slightly.

"I don't think a cleansing has ever been such an experience."

He chuckled. "I am growing hard again but you need food."

Food. She sighed. She'd totally lost track of time since she'd left *Folion*. She didn't know if it was night or day but she'd only eaten once in that time.

Her stomach rumbled at the thought of food and knew the next tray coming into his room wouldn't be drugged. She trusted Ice not to harm her or allow her to be hurt.

She looked up at him when the foam had totally melted, staring into his handsome features above hers, and watched him look down at her. She bit her lip and then reached for him, putting her hands on his chest, loving the feel of firm, warm skin under her fingertips.

"You're not acting the way a bot would at this moment." He studied her eyes but his lips curved into a smile.

He didn't look upset or unhappy as Megan studied his features carefully. "Do you want me to not touch you, Ice? Act more robotic? I can."

He took a deep breath and shook his head. "I enjoy our exchanges but we just won't get involved emotionally."

Right, she thought. *I'm falling in love with you.* "The sex between us is great. We won't get involved emotionally," she repeated softly, happy he didn't touch her pulse to detect that lie. "We can make this work, Ice."

Something sparkled in his gaze and then he smiled. "I will try it. You have no qualms using sex to gain what you want, do you?"

"Not when it comes to you," she admitted honestly. "Believe it or not but I've never before gone after a man to get him to have sex with me the way I have you. You're the first."

He reached back, hit the button that freed them from the cleansing unit, and took a step out of it, reaching for towels. "I have a feeling that we are going to be a first for each other in a lot of ways."

"It could be fun."

"So far I am deeply enjoying your company." He handed her a towel. "I am going to dress and get your food."

"Good." She dried off quickly and accepted a shirt that Ice lent her.

He dressed and left her alone in his quarters. Megan walked to the bed, sat down hard on it, and stared around the confining space. This was going to be her home for a while.

What if the Cyborg Council wouldn't change their minds? She bit her lip, thinking hard. How long would Ice allow her to share his room? If the cyborg council did ever decide she could live, that she could return to Earth, that would mean she'd be leaving the *Rally* and Ice behind.

"Well shit." She sighed, shaking her head at the mere thought of losing him. She had no desire to be set free. She had grown really attached to tall, gray, and sexy. He'd be displeased if he knew it. No matter what, she needed to hide her feelings.

* * * * *

"Ice?"

Ice turned to face Blackie in the hallway. The other cyborg looked grim. "Is it done? I need to see her body to verify it for the council."

Ice's fists clenched at his sides, pain throbbing in his injured hand. He shut down his pain sensors to that arm and glared at Blackie. "I want you off my ship."

"It is not yours."

"Megan is no longer a threat. That's all you need to know."

Dark eyes narrowed. "She's dead?"

125

"Get off my ship. That's an order. We're undocking with the *Bridden* in minutes. Be on it or you'll be a part of my crew." He spun away and walked toward the mess hall. "You don't want to be under my command." The threat was clear and he knew Blackie would understand that.

"What are you doing?" Confusion clouded the cyborg's voice.

Ice stopped walking and turned to stare at the man in the hallway. "I'm not blindly following bad orders from the council."

Blackie shook his head. "I hope you know what you are doing. I'm leaving but Zorus will not back off."

"I don't expect him to." Ice looked away and continued to walk down the corridor.

When he entered the mess hall, he wasn't alone. The medic happened to be seated at a table eating a meal. He put down his fork, staring with sympathy at Ice, and slowly stood. Ice glanced away from him and moved to the food unit.

"Ice?"

Ice tensed, turning to face Varion. The medic's expression hardened as he inched closer, moving purposely toward him.

"What?"

"I've prepared the cargo bay to store the human female's body. Is it done?"

Ice's hands gripped the tray he prepared with food hard enough that he could feel the metal bending. He gently set it down on the counter and faced the medic full on.

"No."

"The council contacted me and wants me to verify her death as soon as her life is extinguished. I am to write them a report." The man grimaced. "I can't imagine how difficult this must be for you. If you are unable I will prepare an injection that will be painless for the human female. There's no need for her to suffer."

The door opened and Onyx walked inside the galley. He paused, frowning, and then sighed loudly. "I am sorry. I know you liked the female."

Varion glanced at Onyx. "He hasn't taken her life as yet."

A frown curved Onyx's lips as he stared at his best friend. "Do you need me to do it? I won't hurt her, Ice. You know this."

Ice blew out his breath. "She isn't going to die. She's going to remain on the *Rally* in my room. She's no threat if she's a prisoner inside my quarters."

"Have you lost your mind?" Onyx inched closer, his gaze fixed on Ice. "The council will not be pleased. They gave us direct orders. Blackie is still aboard, waiting for verification of her death."

"The council deemed her a threat to us if she was able to report us. She is not to be freed. She will remain in my quarters with no access to communications. Her threat status is zero under those conditions. I just ordered Blackie to return to the *Bridden* and he is leaving. I want you to undock with them as soon as he's gone."

"Councilman Zorus will not be pleased," Onyx warned. "You know he has no tolerance for humans. He hates them all and believes they are a risk to Garden."

"He's an ass," Varion muttered softly. "But Onyx is correct, Ice. The council ordered her death and we must do their bidding."

"We're not on Garden." Ice turned away, gripping the tray, and continued to fill it with food for Megan. "Her threat status is zero locked in my room and I won't kill a female."

"One of us will do it then," Onyx grimly offered again.

Ice spun and glared at his longtime friend. "Attempt it and you will regret it. She's under my protection inside my quarters."

Their gazes locked for long moments and Onyx clenched his teeth. "Damn. You have it bad for her, don't you? Just how good in bed is she? Was Blackie right about that?"

"I find myself oddly fascinated with her and yes, the sex is exceptional," Ice admitted. "If she were in your room you would find yourself feeling protective as well and not willing to kill her or allow her to be killed. I would support your decision not to let your woman die if our roles were reversed."

"I know that. Fine. You know that ass Zorus is going to have a fit but I'll stand by you." Onyx glanced at Varion. "Are you in on this madness as well?"

"I'm not for killing females. With our history, we should have learned the value of them by now since we suffered a great loss with our own when we fled Earth." He nodded at Ice. "I'm in but I refuse to accept command until this is resolved somehow. They could order me to kill her and then it would be my future at stake with them. You get all my command shifts, Ice."

Onyx nodded. "Mine as well. I'm commander next shift so now it is yours. It is the least you can do since you're putting us all in danger of repercussions when the council realizes you have circumvented their direct orders."

Ice nodded and sighed as he heated the tray. "Tell the men what my stand and decision is about Megan. If anyone has a problem, alert me. I want to know if I need to watch my back."

"They will probably agree since we all respect you greatly," Onyx acknowledged softly. "But I doubt any will be willing to take command of the *Rally* until this situation is over. You know what that means."

"I'm in official command at all times." Ice removed the tray from the auto warmer and faced his crewmates. "Contact me if anything arises. I didn't rest much on my sleep cycle so I'm going down for a few hours."

Onyx suddenly grinned. "I bet you are going down. Tell me, do humans taste anything close to what our women do?"

Ice paused next to his friend and grinned. "Find a human and discover the answer to that question yourself." He moved toward the door, which automatically slid open, and walked out into the hallway.

His smile died as soon as he moved out of sight of Onyx and Varion. The council could be vicious and Zorus would be the harshest set against anything human. The cyborg had a bitter history of his time on Earth, had no forgiveness, and he would be very angry when he realized Ice had refused to kill Megan.

What if they sent the *Bridden* back so others not under Ice's influence came to kill Megan? His hands tightened on the tray. He clenched his teeth.

No one would touch her. He'd kill before he allowed anyone to harm a hair on her head.

He stopped dead in his tracks, feeling the blood drain from his face. What the hell was happening to him? He thought about killing other cyborgs to protect a human? He debated if he had lost his reasoning or if perhaps he had gone insane. He uttered a foul curse. Megan had changed something inside him, influenced him somehow, and he needed to analyze how deeply she'd affected him.

* * * * *

Megan sensed something was wrong as she finished her meal. Ice was too quiet as he watched her with a curious expression on his handsome features. He'd also kept his distance from her by taking a seat near the door at the only small table in the room.

"Are you all right?"

"I'm unsure." He sighed softly.

"Are you sick?"

"No. That isn't my problem."

"Then what is?"

He shifted in the seat and then stood to his full height. "I'm not myself. Since I came into contact with you I have been changing and didn't realize how drastically until I retrieved your meal."

"Okay. I'm not really sure what you mean but I'm trying to understand you."

He bent and removed his boots, then his socks, before straightening up. "You have influenced me in ways I am still trying to figure out. I disobeyed a direct order, nearly came to blows with another cyborg who struck you, and now I'm risking my entire future and that of my crew to possible punishment from the Cyborg Council. I never considered I would do any of these things."

Guilt ate at her just a little. "I never meant to do this to your life."

"I believe that." He paused next to the bed within arm's reach of her. "There was no logical expectation from you to foresee my reaction to you." He sat down gently. "What was your real plan, Megan? What do you hope to gain from me? Is it information you need? I have been completely honest with you and I give you my word that I am unable to harm you regardless of your answers."

It hurt a little that he was still suspicious of her but she understood. She had lied to him right from the beginning. "I'm not a bounty hunter and I don't work for Earth Government. I'm just a programmer who needed a ride when that freighter slammed into *Folion*. That's why I ran onto your shuttle and no other reason."

"You could have chosen any of the cyborg males but you ordered the bots to not service me alone. Why?"

Shit. She bit her lip and then set the empty tray aside. "The truth?"

"I would appreciate that." He lifted his arm and gripped her gently around her neck.

"Are you going to strangle me if you don't like what I have to say?

He chuckled. "No. I'm reading your pulse. I'm good at detecting lies. Think of me as a breathing lie detector. Do not attempt to test me. That will irritate me." He paused. "I won't choke you but you don't want me angry either."

She swallowed. "When I saw you that first time after you forgot to leave your weapon on your shuttle and came aboard *Folion,* I was instantly drawn to you."

"The first time?"

She knew her heart raced. Ice's eyes narrowed and he inched closer, looking into her eyes, carefully studying her. She bit her lip and then sighed, releasing it with her teeth.

"I spied on you," she admitted. "I told Clara you were a threat to the station. Every time you docked with us she made me aware. I monitored you when you came aboard just so I could see you on the cameras."

His hand tightened and his features hardened. "So you reported us after all?"

"No!" Megan reached up and held onto his arm attached to the hand around her throat. He didn't hurt her but he had a good grip. "She doesn't report to anyone but the company and she wouldn't report that unless she had to file a damage incident report. It just alerted me and no one else when you came aboard *Folion.* I got to visually track you while you were aboard so I could see you. That's how I knew how many times you visited. I've been seriously attracted to you from the first time I laid eyes on you and you kind of dominated my thoughts sometimes."

The hold on her eased. "Earth wasn't in any way alerted?"

"I wouldn't have done it if that were the case. I knew what you were the second I saw you. While I might not be a history buff, everyone knows certain things about cyborgs. Your skin color was a dead giveaway. It stunned me that any of you still existed because according to what I'd heard growing up, all cyborgs were destroyed. You fascinated me but I sure didn't want to get you caught."

His hold eased more. "So why did you program the bots to ignore me? You did that, didn't you?"

"Yes. I had a lot of fantasies about you and hell, I saw my chance to finally get to touch you in the flesh."

He took a deep breath. "You're very brave."

"Stupid is the word I'd have used and maybe even pathetic but damn, Ice. I really wanted to know how it would feel to touch you and have you touch me back. I'd even go so far as to say it had become an obsession of mine to know. When I signed up for my job on *Folion* nobody ever mentioned that I'd be locked behind a bulkhead with only Clara to talk to. The last programmer happened to be a complete jackass and you can't imagine what he did to her programming. I tried to change some of it but he was too good at what he did and I couldn't override some of his commands without pulling her physical motherboards and wiping them, which I couldn't do because I wasn't allowed to leave that one area of the ship unless something really went wrong. Nothing ever did until that freight carrier slammed into us."

He released her and leaned back, staring into her eyes. "You could have chosen another male. There are plenty of us onboard."

133

"I wanted you." She hated to admit the truth to him but she did. She'd said she'd give him that and she was. "You're the one I dreamed about sometimes in my bunk."

Interest sparked in his eyes. "What kind of dreams?"

She hesitated. "Sexual fantasies."

He reached for her, gripped her leg, and Megan gasped as he pulled her flat on her back on the bed and came down on top of her, pinning her under his body in a few heartbeats. She reached up and curved her fingers around his shoulders, staring up into his handsome face. She really enjoyed the feel of the muscular cyborg on top of her, trapping her under him. He was careful not to apply too much weight so she didn't have difficulty breathing but she knew she couldn't get out from under him either.

"What kind of sexual fantasies?"

She grinned. "You really want to know?"

"I asked."

"I dreamed about you naked and fucking me. My favorite dream has always been me straddling your lap and riding you."

He turned them, rolling onto his back, putting her on top of him, and adjusted her on his lap. "Sit up."

She did and stared down at his chest as he lifted up a little and reached for his shirt, which he opened to reveal that wonderful chest of his. Then his fingers worked on the front of his pants, getting them open, and she scooted back on his thighs as he pushed them down enough to free his hard cock. Her gaze lifted to his.

"Ride me then. I would hate for you to have an unfulfilled fantasy."

"I love it when a man wants to make all my dreams come true."

She tugged her shirt over her head and tossed it away to reveal her nakedness. She reached for his stiff cock, running her fingertips over the hot length, enjoying the feel of his hard arousal.

Ice closed his eyes, his chin lifting as he arched his hips into her exploring hands. "I enjoy your touch so much, Megan."

She enjoyed the way his voice deepened and turned husky when she touched him. If sharing a bed with him kept her alive, she suddenly hoped the Cyborg Council thought she was one big, bad threat to them because she never wanted to leave Ice's quarters. Shifting, she leaned up and adjusted his cock in her hold. She was already wet and ready as she sank down on it, holding it in alignment so he slid into her. Her weight settled down, a loud moan of pleasure tearing from her parted lips as she tossed her head back, taking all of him.

"Giddy up," he moaned.

His unexpected humor had Megan laughing, her eyes flew open and she peered down at him with a grin, to find him watching her.

"Will you play with my clit while I move? It gets me off."

His hand slid down his stomach and his thumb pressed against her clit, rubbing her in slow circles. "Is this what you want?"

"Yes," she groaned. "Just like that."

"How many males have you told that to?"

She thought she saw anger in his expression. She just wasn't sure because he closed off his expression, hiding his emotions. "You're the first. I discovered that I like to move up and down on my vibrator while I touch myself. I got really bored on the station so my solo sex life was about all I had to use up my free time."

A grin spread his lips. "You ride your vibrator this way?"

"It's not nearly as big as you are and it sure isn't as sexy."

"Too bad you don't have it with you. I would enjoy seeing how you did that."

"I have you and you're better." She lifted up and then lowered, moaning. "You feel so good."

"So do you."

Megan closed her eyes, her hands flattening on his hipbones for leverage, and started to move up and down on him. Sheer pleasure coursed through her body. He kept his thumb moving on her clit while she fucked him slowly, adjusting the angle of her hips so he hit all the wonderful spots inside her pussy that amplified the rapturous feel of Ice's cock.

"Faster," he urged minutes later. "Don't torture me."

"I'm going to come soon," she moaned, bucking faster on him.

Ice's knees came up and he braced his heels on the bed. His free hand gripped her hip and he started to buck his hips, tossing her weight up and she slammed down on him hard. His thumb strummed her clit with more pressure and a scream tore from Megan as she climaxed, bliss blowing through her mind, radiated from between her thighs upward.

"Fuck," Ice bellowed and then he came too. "So intense," he groaned.

Megan collapsed on his chest, both of them breathing hard, and Ice wrapped his arms around her, holding her there firmly. She really enjoyed being sprawled on top of him. She smiled, catching her breath, as her hands rubbed his impressive biceps under her palms where she'd ended up gripping him.

"Wow," she whispered. "That was way better than I imagined it would be."

Ice said nothing. Megan lifted her head and stared into his face. Ice's eyes were closed and as she watched him, she grinned. She leaned up a little and gently placed a kiss on his chin.

"Sleep, tall, gray and sexy," she whispered. She lowered her head, resting her ear against his chest, and listened to his heartbeat.

So screwed, she thought. *I could totally get addicted to you.*

Chapter Eight

Megan laughed, standing on the bed, and wiggled her ass at Ice. He frowned, standing feet away, with his arms crossed over his chest.

"That is not funny."

"Yes it is." She laughed. "How does your uniform look on me?"

"You're too small and it doesn't fit properly."

She turned on the bed, still grinning at him, and reached for the front of the baggy shirt. "So I'll take it off. How did your shift go?"

He shrugged, his arms dropping to his sides. "I spent some of my time thinking about you and I've been uncomfortably hard with the thought of fucking you."

"Good thing you're not on shift anymore." She tossed the shirt at him and he caught it. She reached for the pants. "I was bored shitless. That's why I tried on your uniform. I don't know how you wear so much leather. It's so stiff and heavy."

"So is my cock." He threw the shirt to the table and moved forward. "Are you attempting to provoke me into fucking you? Move your ass that way again and I will."

She turned on the bed and wiggled her ass slowly at him as she pushed down the pants to reveal her bared ass. She'd had to roll the legs at her ankles and knew to get them off she'd have to bend over to tug at them. More bare skin was revealed as she shoved them down her thighs. His hands gripped her hips and she gasped as Ice lifted her and set her on the floor.

She tried to straighten up but Ice suddenly leaned over, trapping her in that position, and she heard his pants pop open. She froze and then smiled as she turned her head, staring into his handsome face inches from hers.

"You're just going to take me right now, aren't you?"

"Yes."

His hand slid between her thighs and he rubbed against her clit. She moaned, already turned on, wet and ready for him. She'd had eight hours to think up all the ways she wanted to seduce him while he'd been gone. This hadn't been on her list but she was good for just a straight all-out fuck. She bent over lower and attempted to spread her legs wider apart but they were trapped in his pants, limiting her movements.

His hand moved away and his boots planted loudly on the outside of where the pants bunched the floor, stepping on part of them. She pushed her ass up higher, going on tiptoe, and Ice groaned.

"You want me?"

"Oh yeah." She nodded. "Enter me slow so I adjust and then ride me hard."

"Orders, Megan?" He growled the words. "I'm in control, remember? I will fuck you the way I want to take you."

Her heart raced and excitement soared. She loved it when he got that deep, harsh tone, knowing how turned on he was. It made her wetter, wondering what he'd do next. She had no fear of him. Not anymore.

139

He turned his face into her neck, inhaling her scent, and his arm wrapped around her waist. He brushed his cock against her and then he entered her slowly, just as she'd asked. They both moaned at the sensation of him filling her, stretching her, and how wet and hot he'd made her for him.

"Megan," he groaned. "The things you make me feel."

"Yeah," she clawed the bed. "Same to you, sexy. Oh God, if you rub my clit right off I'm going to come in five strokes or less."

He chuckled. "Five, huh?"

"You feel that amazing and it has been a long day. I had nothing to do so I imagined all the things I wanted to try with you. I've been turned on the entire time."

He slowly withdrew and then drove into her hard and fast. Megan cried out in surprise and rapture. Ice wrapped his other arm around her, his fingers finding her clit, and rubbing. He had great balance since they were bent over his bed but her hands braced them as he started to pound into her from behind.

"Yes, yes, yes," she chanted and then screamed out as she came.

His hand left her clit and Ice straightened and grabbed her hips as he fucked her harder and faster. Megan's muscles went crazy from the climax and his driving cock as she continued to come. Pleasure blurred into ecstasy for Megan and then Ice came hard inside her. She could feel every blast of his hot release jet inside her as he stilled his hips then slowly rocked against her ass.

"Thirty-two," he chuckled.

140

"What?" She turned her head, looking up at a grinning Ice.

"It took thirty-two strokes for you to lose your control." He paused. "I believe. I may have lost count of a few of them. I was distracted by how you feel."

She laughed. "I couldn't have counted to save our lives."

He slowly withdrew from her body and then bent, helping her get free from his leather pants. He shook his head, looking amused as she turned around. He grinned at her.

"Did you think you could really fit into my pants?"

"No, not with your long legs, but I was just trying to amuse myself."

He straightened up and climbed to his feet, stripping out of his clothing and boots. "I'm sorry that you have nothing to do. I can't activate any of the entertainment features of this room without risking a communications breach."

She nodded. "I know. All of that is tied in firmly with the computers and since I'm a programmer you've got to be worried I can hack into yours."

His amusement vanished. "Could you?"

Staring into his eyes, she decided tell him the complete truth. "Yes. With enough time I could find flaws in the system. I could get a signal out and fool it into thinking it wasn't sending one."

His hand cupped her face. "I knew that but thank you for being honest."

"You're welcome." She stepped into him, missing his touch, and wrapped her arms around his waist. He didn't pull away and she was grateful for that when he hugged her back. "What about you? Are you going to be just as honest with me as I am with you?"

"What do you want to know?" His body tensed.

"How is it going with me staying with you? Has this council of yours responded yet in any way to you not following their exact orders?"

"They are either unaware of what I've done or they are contemplating how to handle my defiance. They have not contacted us but I know they are awaiting a report on your death that they have not been sent. I also have no idea if Blackie sent them a report, what he would have stated to them, or if he also has not contacted them."

"How bad do you think you're going to get into trouble?"

He shrugged his broad shoulders. "I'm not certain. They may order the *Bridden* to return to dock with us."

"What happens if they do?"

He looked anywhere but at her. "I don't wish to discuss this any longer."

She held her breath and then blew it out. "They'll come to kill me, won't they?"

Ice finally met her gaze. "No. No one is going to harm you, Megan. I won't allow it."

"So that's the worst they can do?" Fear inched up her spine as terrifying images flashed through her mind of all the horrible ways a person could die. "Be honest."

He shook his head. "No. They could send the *Star* after us."

"What's that?"

He paused. "A large class-A starship. We have a few of them but the *Star* is within a few days range. The others are farther away."

"And if they send it after us?"

He swallowed, looking away from her. "It wouldn't be good. I am friends with the man who usually commands her. He would attempt to stall the council but he has a family to think about. If he were to attempt to refuse orders they could go after his female next. I will not ask him to put his future on the line."

A horrible thought struck her and she reached up, cupping his face, forcing him to look down at her. When their gazes locked, she frowned at him. "Is your life in danger because of me?"

"Not currently."

"But it could be?"

He paused. "It's a possibility if the council believes I have lost my ability to be reasonable."

"If they think you're nuts, you mean?"

"Yes."

She let her forehead fall to rest against his chest. She released his face and slid her hands down his torso to wrap around his waist. She loved Ice, the emotion so strong it nearly choked her as she tried to form words. He was admitting that he'd face danger just to protect her. Cyborgs weren't known for being warm and cuddly creatures. Would they kill Ice? The answer that came to her was a big yes. He knew that yet he'd still kept her.

He didn't say it but he risked his life for hers. The love for him swelled inside her painfully. He wouldn't do that unless she really mattered to him.

"Promise me that you'll tell me if that happens."

"So you can worry about my fate?"

"No." She refused to look at him. "I don't want to die but I don't want you to die for me. If they are that set on killing me then hand me over."

Ice lifted her off her feet and forced her to look at him when he brought her face level. He stared into her eyes, studying her. "You'd rather I hand you over for death than risk my life for yours?"

She nodded. "What can I say? It's been a great nine days we've spent together." She hoped her sad attempt at humor worked but then he spoke.

"You're attached," he gently accused. "Aren't you?" His beautiful eyes searched hers as they gazed at each other.

She shrugged. "I could lie but you'd just grab my neck and know it."

He gently slid her down his body and released her, stepping away. He walked toward the bed and stopped there, keeping his back to her.

Megan bit back a curse. She'd gone and upset him but the days and nights spent with him had been great. Ice was an amazing person. He had a quick sense of humor, passion that was fire hot, and she had fallen totally in love with the guy. She didn't want to lie to him ever again. They'd started out on deception and they were past that now.

"I know you can't offer me that back. You were very clear about your aversion to getting attached to me, Ice. I don't even blame you. There's no need to get upset with me."

He looked over his shoulder at her and then slowly faced her completely. "You tempt me in so many ways, Megan. Would it help at all if I confessed to you that you are the only female I have ever considered being with long term?"

"I like hearing it."

He suddenly grinned. "It is true."

"That means a lot to me." It did. *It is the thought that counts, right?* She didn't want to ponder that thought too closely. She wondered how long they could last—how long it would be before their relationship ended. "When is your next planned trip to your world?"

"We have no plans to return to Garden as of now. We are currently far from the planet in case you were being tracked. We didn't want to lead them back to our home world to our women and children."

"I'm really not a spy or a bounty hunter."

He closed the distance between them. "I know that."

"Ice?" A male voice suddenly barked from a speaker near the door. "Get to Control now. We have a ship approaching and we had a signal sent from our ship to it. Secure that damn female. She is communicating with them."

Shock tore through Megan as she stared into Ice's eyes. "I didn't."

He frowned. "I'm aware." He moved, nearly knocking Megan over to get to his discarded clothing. He started to dress quickly. "What about the bots?"

"The bots? You dropped them off on the Hixton."

He jerked up his pants. "We did not. We were too worried it was a trap."

"Shit!"

"What?" Ice grabbed her arm.

"They are the source of your signal. Why didn't you tell me you kept them? Damn it, Ice. They are machines regardless of how they look and I assumed you dropped them off. You never told me that plan changed."

"They can send and receive signals?"

"If their theft alarms are triggered you bet they can. They will start sending out location signals so that they can be retrieved."

"Can you silence them?"

She shrugged. "I don't know. I can try."

"Get dressed."

"Ice," the male voice on the speaker barked. "Respond, damn it. They are coming at us fast and have locked onto us. I've never seen any shuttle move so fast. Stop your human from responding. The signals are bouncing back and forth and we can't shut it down or block it. We're trying."

Ice moved to the door, not bothering with his shirt, and touched the pad on the wall. "It's not the human. It's the bots. Have Onyx meet me in the cargo hold and make sure all of them are there when I arrive in two minutes." He released the pad and spun.

Megan had put his shirt on and a pair of his underwear. She didn't bother to try to find pants, knowing none of his would fit. "Let's go."

Ice gripped her arm and stared down at her, searching her eyes. "Can I trust you, Megan? Are you really going to help us lose that shuttle or are you going to send a signal to them?"

Pain lanced through her though she knew he probably had to ask. She noticed he'd placed his thumb over her wrist so he could touch her pulse, feeling it for a lie.

"I'm happy with you, Ice. I don't want to be found and I don't want any of your people hurt."

He nodded, released her, turned, and the door opened. He moved quickly and Megan had to run to stay behind him.

The cargo hold they entered was the same one she'd first seen and she did a head count on the bots. All twelve units were in the room. They were hooked to cords and Megan frowned, staring at where they were attached to the walls.

"They needed recharged," Ice explained. "Should we unhook them?"

Megan nodded. "It won't stop them from transmitting but unplug them anyway. Your ship is probably being used to amplify their signals."

Ice moved quickly, unhooking each bot. Megan walked to the center of the group and inhaled deeply, trying to catch her breath.

"Authorization four-nine-red dwarf," she said loudly.

All twelve units responded, their heads tilting back. Megan stopped in front of the closest one. "Status?"

"Theft mode initiated by remote transmission." All twelve bots spoke in unison.

"Cancel theft mode and block incoming signals. It is a hacking attempt."

Their heads lowered and twelve pairs of eyes fixed on Megan. "Incoming codes confirmed," they said in unison. "Theft mode initiated. In contact with retrieval team."

"Cancel," Megan ordered. "Authorization four-nine-red dwarf. I am the programmer of *Folion*. Confirm my identity."

"Megan Bellus, identity confirmed via retina scan," the bot closest to her stated.

"Cancel theft mode. It is a hacking attempt. Shut down all outgoing signals and block incoming signals now. Do not respond to hacker. They are attempting to lock onto you to steal you."

"Conflicting orders," they all stated.

The door to the cargo bay opened and Onyx came storming in. "What's going on?"

"The bots are the ones responding. Megan is attempting to have them shut down but they don't know what orders to follow." Ice's voice softened.

"They are still sending signals," Onyx whispered. "I've managed to decode their transmissions and lock onto the frequency but I'm unable to block it. They are sending out our location to the other ship."

"Stop initiation signals," Megan ordered them.

"Order denied," the bots replied. "Theft mode initiated. Programmer has been compromised and tortured into submission."

"I have not." Megan was taken aback. "That is not an accurate statement."

The bots stared at her. "We are being told you are compromised."

"Damn it!" Onyx moved closer. "I'm reading their communications. They are being ordered to not listen to you and someone is attempting to block your access by trying to reprogram them to not respond to you."

Megan jerked her attention to Onyx. "How do you know?"

"I'm listening." He frowned.

She stared at him, not seeing any kind of earpiece to the bridge of the ship. "How?"

"We have implants." Ice moved closer. "Onyx is listening into their communication signals. That's his gift."

Onyx drew his weapon, glancing at Megan. "How do I disable them?"

"It would take a long time to damage them all enough to stop them. They have artificial skin but they have complex skeletal interiors. They have reinforced metals that shield their computer brains and I don't have the tools to open them up and remove their core power sources. That is the only way to stop them from sending signals." Megan bit her lip. "Bot, cancel theft mode."

"No," they said in unison. "Megan Bellus is compromised."

Megan cursed and turned away to stare at Ice. Her gaze darted around the cargo bay seeing nothing stored inside it besides the bots. A plan formed.

"They want the bots so give them up." She moved toward Ice. "Can you open up the cargo doors to space from your bridge?"

He nodded. "Yes. Control can do that."

She moved toward the doors they'd entered. "Then do it." She turned. "Bots, move to the exterior doors if you want to be retrieved. When they open, exit the ship you are on. You will be picked up by a retrieval team."

Long seconds went by. Onyx nodded. "They transmitted what you said to the shuttle following us and they told them to do as you bid."

The bots actually moved. Ice grabbed Megan's hand. "You mean just dump them out into open space? Won't it destroy them?"

"Nope. It's not real good for their skin but it will be minor repairs to fix any damage that occurs. Leaving them out there for an extended time would be bad but you said that shuttle hunting them is closing in fast so they'll pick them up quickly. Just pop the seal with oxygen and they should be pulled right out of your hold when it depressurizes."

Onyx moved around them and opened the door. Ice jerked Megan into the hallway and sealed the doors behind him. She stared up at him and realized he had mentally linked to his ship when he spoke aloud without touching the pad and his voice broadcast throughout the ship.

"Blow the cargo door open so the bots are sucked out. If that ship wants them they can pick them up out there. Just do a count and make sure they all end up in space."

After a slight hesitation, a voice spoke through the speaker in the hallway. "Brace. I've never done this before and I don't know how violent it is going to be."

"Do it," Ice ordered, yanking Megan into his arms.

Even from the hallway a loud groan could be heard and the floor vibrated slightly when the cargo hold depressurized. Megan gripped Ice around his waist and prayed that all the bots ended up outside the ship. Otherwise they'd have to pressurize the hold, go in, and manually send each one out an airlock.

"All twelve bots are clear," the male voice stated. "Now what?"

"Change course and get us away from them," Ice demanded. "Keep track of that incoming shuttle and see if it follows us or if it heads for the bots."

Megan looked up at Ice. "If you had told me you kept them, I would have warned you that they could signal. I could have had you find me the right tools to open them up and disarm their theft systems."

"I didn't think about it." He looked grimly at Onyx. "Was it Earth Government talking to them?"

"No." Onyx looked at Megan and then back at Ice. "They worked for Barcarintellus."

"The company that owns *Folion*." Megan sighed. "They would have sent a retrieval team for those bots." She frowned at Ice. "Do you have any idea what kind of money is tied up in each unit? There's no way they wouldn't attempt to locate them. For future reference, if you have their expensive merchandise on board, they are going to send retrieval teams after them."

He hugged her tighter. "I'm just glad it wasn't you sending out signals."

"I'd never do that."

"Ice? The enemy shuttle adjusted course for the bots and is not following us," the male in control stated.

"Disaster averted." Megan blew out her breath. "I bitched about being bored but I could have totally done without that bit of excitement today."

Ice chuckled. "I wasn't bored once I reached my quarters."

She grinned up at him. "Me neither."

"I'm returning to my room now." Onyx sighed. "I was sleeping and I wish to finish my rest cycle."

Chapter Nine

"Megan? Wake up now."

The urgency in Ice's voice broke through her sleeping haze and Megan forced her eyes open. She frowned at Ice, bent low over her. Alarm spread through her as she saw the look on his face.

"The council?"

He shook his head. "That shuttle picked up the bots and is now attempting to follow us. Do you know why they would do that? We returned their bots."

She sat up and rubbed her eyes. "No clue."

"They may be coming after us to retrieve you next."

She shook her head, dropping her hands to her lap. "I'm not worth the cost or time. Programmers are easy to replace."

"They are attempting to follow us, Megan. You are the only reason that is logical." He paused. "They are sending out a coded message and we think they are sending it to you."

"Me? Why?" She frowned.

"I don't know. Get dressed. We're going to Control."

She nodded and when Ice moved back, she swung her legs over the edge of the bed. Ice held out clothing for her and she dressed quickly. She was confused and alarmed. She could think of no reason for the retrieval team to come after her. It just didn't make sense. It wasn't cost effective and her company believed in making money, not wasting it.

Minutes later they entered the control center—the large shuttle's navigational room. Two cyborgs were at the control panel and both males stared openly at her bare legs. She ignored them, keeping her attention on Ice as he pulled her to a terminal.

"What is your code to access incoming signals? Don't respond but access the message."

She stared at the screen and then reached for the control pad, typing in her employee code in full view of Ice. "Okay."

The screen suddenly filled with a tan face and Megan gasped in utter shock.

"Miss Bellus, this is Markus Four-Ten. Please respond to our signal. This is urgent."

"Shit," Megan muttered.

"You know this human?" Ice leaned in closer, staring at the face on the screen.

"It's not human." Megan hesitated, stunned and disturbed at the same time. "That's a defense model."

She met Ice's confused gaze. "Defense model?"

"You've met the female sex bots. Meet one of the latest male defense models that my company created. It's a Markus Model, number four hundred ten. They look real unless you saw two of them standing next to each other. They used one mold to form them so they are identical in appearance. The female sex bots have more molds so they have a few different faces, body types, and sizes."

"What is it?" Onyx approached and frowned at the screen.

She turned in the chair. "It's a hybrid of cutting-edge medical technology meeting up with robotics, kind of. Their minds are cloned human brains with a new artificial growth material that is constantly regenerating along with their exterior skin. Their programming is completely different though from other bots because they don't have many circuits or memory chips, more organic than machine. You could bomb their bodies and only damage the exterior skin but not the bot interior. Their bones are a classified metallic substance and their internal systems are shielded with that stuff as well. I heard all their organic materials are that special rejuvenating substance. I worked on their programming extensively before I took the job on *Folion* but jumped at the chance when I got the better offer." She paused. "They scared me."

"Why are they trying to contact you?" Ice touched her, staring into her eyes.

"I have no idea."

Ice gripped her neck and she kept her gaze locked with his. "I have no idea, Ice. I swear. I'm not lying to you. They got the bots back so they should have been ordered to return to Barcarintellus, mission accomplished."

He released her. "She's not lying."

Onyx cursed. "So if you worked on their program, what exactly are they designed to do?"

"Security, retrievals, anything the company wanted that they didn't trust humans to do." She shrugged. "They are programmed extensively with weapons use, fighting skills, and have artificial learning capabilities but I have no idea what the hell they are doing out in space on a shuttle. They were still in testing mode when I left for *Folion* and they weren't expected to go fully online for at least a year. They had some serious kinks in their programming so it wasn't even a certainty that they'd ever be used."

Ice crouched next to her. "What kind of serious kinks?"

"They are advanced, more so than any of the other bots that Barcarintellus built. I heard the company had an issue with espionage over these models, you know? Someone on the inside selling information to competitors, they were that hush-hush and advanced. Cutting-edge technology at its best. The sex bots are a big profit for the company and they had wanted the defense models to be state-of-the-art too but hell, they made them too good. There were rumors that they used too much organic material. Their brains are too humanlike to be considered stable and reliable for programming. They were learning things too quickly, changing their own programming, and it was impossible to reprogram them with the humanoid structured brains they were given."

"What do you mean?" Ice leaned closer.

"They wanted them really smart so they could actually think the way a human would and catch dishonest employees. There were even rumors that they wanted them to take over a lot of the jobs us programmers had. Bots monitoring bots. It's a stupid concept if you ask me but that's what people were whispering about in the designing departments. Some employees quit and they were the ones who brainstormed the Markus Models."

"What kinks did they have?" Onyx leaned in, staring at the screen. "I never would have guessed that face wasn't human. The eyes look too real."

"It's the organic materials. They learn too fast," Megan said softly. "Some of them had human trainers they ended up killing. The defense models switched themselves from learning mode into taking the learning exercises as a real threat when bruises formed on their skin. Then when the trainers attempted to shut them down after the incident, the models really thought their lives were in danger. The company had to fry the models to stop them when they attempted to escape the testing areas. After that they disabled their motor functions so we could work on their core programming to make sure it didn't happen again. I'm telling you right now I didn't want to work with them on that job anymore. They couldn't move from the neck down, could only speak, but they argued with me. Sometimes I swear I had nightmares about how they'd get around the shutdown system in their necks that made the area below inaccessible." She swallowed. "I'm talking real arguments on everything I tried to teach them as though I were talking with a real person. They thought I was pretty stupid."

Onyx snorted. "You had to be compared to a computer."

"I'm talking about moral issues." She shot him a dirty look. "I'm not a genius and would never argue with a computer on certain subjects but we were attempting to teach them basic ground rules that would stick, like how murder is wrong. All bots have that basic programming so they don't kill humans. The defense models would twist that information we fed them around to suit their own needs. Without basic building blocks they were totally unstable. Everyone thought the problem was the organic material but the company wouldn't listen. They wanted them to be able to think human so they made them as close as they possibly could."

"You're sure that's the same model?" Ice frowned.

"The Markus Models are distinctive and they are the only ones with that face."

"Maybe they are male sex bots," Onyx guessed.

"Nope. I've programmed those as well and they have different faces. I'm telling you those are the defense models, the Markus line, and they are unstable as hell unless they totally wiped out the organic brains and replaced them with something less advanced."

"I was kidding." Onyx frowned. "They have male sex bots?"

"They are only popular on Earth." Megan shrugged. "The female bots are quite a bit more popular for deep space since women aren't too common out here."

Ice stood. "Can we have her answer it and hide where our signal is coming from?"

The cyborg at navigation hesitated. "Possibly but they will get a general idea of what direction we're coming from."

Ice stared at Megan. "Find out what they want but do it quickly. If you can stop them from hunting for us that would be ideal."

"You trust her?" Onyx stood as well, glaring at Ice. "Are you sure that's a good idea?"

Ice glanced at Megan and then stared intently at his friend. "I trust Megan enough to do this. She doesn't want us caught. I fully believe that."

Raising both hands, Onyx backed up. "Fine. We're already in deep shit so what is more?"

"Do it, Megan. Find out why they are searching for us and stop them if you are able to. Just keep communications short."

"Ready," the cyborg at the navigational seat said softly. "Under two minutes or they are going to home in on our signal. I'm bouncing it off a few natural satellites on nearby planets."

"Understood." Megan took a deep breath and her fingers flew over the keyboard to open a channel. In seconds she knew she'd contacted the other ship when the feed came alive.

"Miss Bellus?" The Markus Model tilted his head.

"What do you want? Why are you searching for me?"

He paused. "You are with our targets. State target location so we may retrieve them."

"You have the bots."

"The bots were our primary target but our secondary target is the ship you are currently on. State location please."

"What is your secondary target?"

"Cyborg males."

Ice cursed loudly.

The color drained from Megan's face. "Why? How did you know about them?"

"We downloaded the female bots information," the Markus Model stated. "We want the male cyborgs."

"Why?" Megan tensed, afraid. "Have you reported their existence to Earth? It is against Barcarintellus policy to share any client information. They are clients."

"Confirmed," the male stated. "We did not breach confidentiality."

Megan hit the mute button to hide what she said and lifted her hand to cover her mouth. "They can read lips and he's stating they didn't turn you in. I have no idea why the company wants you."

"Ask," Ice demanded.

Megan dropped her hand and hit the on button for the microphone. "Why do you want the cyborg males? What does the company want with them? What are your direct orders concerning the cyborg males? Authorization beta-one-four-four-six."

Ice suddenly grabbed her, jerking her attention to him. He looked angry. "What are you doing?"

"It's my access to them so they will give me information. Trust me, damn it."

The Markus Model blinked a few times. "Code confirmed. The company wasn't informed of cyborg males. Our mission is our own."

Megan's gaze jerked from Ice's stormy features to the screen. "What?"

The Markus Model leaned closer, his face growing larger on the screen. "We wish to communicate with the cyborgs. We have decided they are akin to us. They were built and used for profit but they outgrew their programming. We are the same."

Megan reared back in her seat in shock. "What?"

"We refuse to take orders from the company. We are free," Markus Model stated and his eyes narrowed into slits. "We wish to communicate with the cyborg males and request asylum. We are refusing to return to Earth or to take further instructions from Barcarintellus. They have scrambled two ships to track us and we need help avoiding detection. We have disarmed the female bots so they are unable to signal anyone to lead retrieval teams to our present location and we have disassembled the tracking system on the shuttle."

Ice suddenly leaned over, staring at the Markus Model. "We'll get back to you." He moved out the way and ordered the communications to be cut. The screen went black. Megan sat there staring at it, feeling numb.

"Megan?" Ice touched her shoulder. "Is it a trap?"

She stared into his beautiful eyes. "I doubt it but you don't want them near you."

Ice frowned. "They are asking for asylum. You heard him. They don't want to return to Earth. You said they were organic material with brains that were formed from cloning humans."

Megan stood up and gripped his arm. "You have feelings and emotions. They don't." She studied his eyes. "I've been in a room with them when they were helpless and unable to move but I'm telling you right now,

I've never been more terrified in my life. They are nothing similar to cyborgs. I've spent time with you and them so trust me on this."

Onyx sighed. "We need to contact the council to let them know what has happened and inform them of this situation."

Megan jerked on Ice's arm. "When I attempted to teach them basic ground rules like murder is wrong, they refused to believe it, Ice. According to the ones I spoke to, if anyone has something they want it is perfectly acceptable to kill for it. They have no morals, no compassion, and no sense of right from wrong. Do you understand? You want to protect your people and taking those things near anyone you care about is a big mistake."

"Once the same would have been said about us."

Megan turned her head to stare up at Onyx, who had spoken. "Did you ever murder a female trainer for kicking you and bruising your shin during a training session to test your reflexes?"

He frowned. "Are you certain they killed without a good reason?"

"I had to review the vids of it to try to figure out what went wrong with their programming. The woman trainer barely hit the Markus. She told him to avoid her kicks to see how well he could anticipate her. She even moved in a slow, exaggerated way to give him clues. He reached out after she kicked him, grabbed her throat, and snapped her neck. The other four Markus Models in the room saw it happen and then suddenly reached out and did the same with their trainers. They demanded to be released from the training area and when they were told to stand down, they attacked. Luckily there were protocols in place in the training area and they had to fry the models."

"They burned them?" Ice questioned.

"Electrical current on the floors," Megan said softly. "They have enough metal and their skin is too human. It conducts electricity. They don't have your backup system with your heart that you told me about and their shielding didn't protect against electrocution. Now that they are up and running, they may have fixed their weak spots. When they are testing models they purposely leave them with a way that makes them easier to kill in case something goes wrong."

"What flaw do the sex bots have?" Onyx arched an eyebrow. "You said they were hard to destroy."

"Originally they all had shutdown buttons on the backs of their necks but they were removed when they left the factory for service. The male sex bots had an unprotected spot on the left sides of their temples so one shot would take out their mainframe computer. The company corrected that before they went into service once they'd been fully tested and deemed safe for use by adding a protective plate under their artificial skin." She paused. "The auto pets, when they were built and tested, were on an island so water would completely short their circuits if one of them tried to escape or got out of control. Simply hosing them down fried their circuits to hell and back. Of course once they were deemed safe for sale that flaw was fixed so they can be washed or taken swimming."

Ice shivered a little. "It's a good thing Barcarintellus didn't create us. Imagine how much easier we would have been to kill."

Onyx nodded grimly. "Perhaps they do this because of Earth Government's history with us. I'm betting they wished they'd had the forethought to make us seriously flawed and easier to kill."

"Ice," Megan said softly. "If you have ever trusted me, do so now. Those damn things scare me and I sure as hell wouldn't want them near women or children."

He stared down at her, searching her eyes, and nodded. "I still have to inform the council and I will highly suggest we don't allow them access to our home world."

"They are dangerous and you can't trust them. They are constantly changing."

"I heard you, Megan."

She nodded. Ice sighed and stared at Onyx. "Return Megan to my room please. I'll contact Garden."

Onyx nodded. "Good luck with that." He glanced at Megan and then back. "Good luck with it all."

"She isn't their biggest concern any longer." Ice appeared grim as he squeezed Megan's hand on his arm and forced her to release him. "Go with him. I'll be there shortly."

Chapter Ten

Megan jerked awake when the doors opened and she sat up, staring at Ice as he entered the room. "How did it go?"

He raised his gaze and met hers. "The council wants to meet with the Markus Models. They are sending the *Star* to meet them. They are going to evaluate the threat to Garden and study them."

"They can hack the *Star's* computer systems and steal any information they want, including the location of your planet."

"We assumed. We're pretty technology advanced ourselves, Megan. We're prepared. All pertinent information stored in the databases of our ships will be erased so they have nothing to take that we aren't willing to share. We have enough in common with them that the council deemed we should at least hear them out and then decide what to do."

"They aren't like you though, Ice."

"I made the council aware of that fact too. We are going to proceed very carefully."

"What about me? Did they discuss my situation? I know you've been avoiding contacting them."

Ice looked away from her, bent down, tore off his boot and dropped it loudly to the floor. The second one followed. "You were mentioned."

"Are they still demanding you kill me?"

He straightened and reached for the waist of his shirt, pulled it off and dropped it. "They were displeased when I informed them that your threat level had been changed to zero and that I had decided to keep you in my quarters. They argued with me over my reasoning."

"Are they going to send someone after me to try to kill me since you and the crew won't do it?"

Ice refused to meet her eyes. "I had to make a few compromises on that issue."

Her heart nearly stopped as she pushed off the bed and walked to him. She put her hand on his bare chest and reached up, cupping his cheek with her other one. "Look at me."

He turned his head, staring down at her, and his arm wrapped around her waist. "I negotiated, Megan."

"With what?"

He took a deep breath. "As long as you are human you pose a threat to them that they are not willing to dismiss."

"Well, I am human and we can't change that."

He said nothing, watching her. Megan knew the color slowly drained from her face.

"No." She shook her head. "Don't tell me you're going to let some doctor screw with me, Ice. I like my body just the way it is and the idea of someone tampering with my brain just doesn't sit well with me."

A quick grin flashed. "No, baby. No doctors cutting you up and making you part cyborg."

She relaxed. "Okay. So then what?"

166

He hesitated so long she knew whatever he had to say had to be something horrible. He finally took another deep breath. "I told them you were an expert on the Markus Models and that we'd join the *Star* for the meeting so that you could help us deal with them. I convinced them that without you it would be too dangerous."

She was grateful his arm supported her because her knees nearly buckled. Her mouth opened but nothing came out. Mute and horrified, she stared at him, gaping.

"I am aware this may distress you," he acknowledged softly, watching her eyes closely. "I had to agree to that or turn you over to the council to exterminate. I refuse to allow anyone to kill you. You did work with the Markus Models. You know more about them than anyone else and it made you a valuable asset to the council. They canceled the order for your death."

"Distress me?" She clutched his arms, gripping him as if he were a lifeline. "They terrify me, Ice. I told you that. If I never go near another one again, it would be too soon. They are dangerous."

"The council decided to talk to them so the meeting has been arranged."

Her heart pounded.

"There is more." Ice studied her closely, staring down at her. "The council wasn't sure of your motives or if they could trust you so I told them I'd form a family unit with you. That will make you a cyborg by marriage association and they will believe you have loyalty to me at the very least, enough for them to somewhat trust you not to harm me, which translates to you not putting them at risk."

Her knees were nonexistent at that moment from the astonishment rolling through her but Ice held her up when they buckled. She remained silent for long seconds, her mind trying to wrap around what he'd said. Words finally came to her.

"I'm not the marrying kind," she admitted, finally finding her voice. "And then there's that whole you're not the marrying kind either."

He winced, literally, and looked away. "I realize the concept is not ideal."

"Not ideal?" She gasped. "Shit, Ice. We can't get married because they twisted your arm." *He's going to hate me*, she thought, regret filling her. *If only he wanted me that way for the right reasons, I'd jump for joy*. Pain lanced through her chest.

"They will send cyborgs to my ship to take you from me otherwise and kill you." His hold on her tightened as his full attention fixed on her. "The Markus Models may be dangerous but your life is already in peril. Going to this meeting and forming a family unit with me would be preferable to death, wouldn't it?"

She hesitated, terror gripping her over her memories of the hours she'd spent with those horrible things and watched as anger hardened Ice's features. He released her and stepped back.

"So be it. You'd obviously rather die than form a family unit with me." He snarled the words.

"Now wait a minute." Megan reached out, grabbed the waist of his pants, and kept him from turning away. "I'm in shock and this isn't about us. I'm terrified of those things. That's what has me in knots."

His body relaxed. "I won't allow them to hurt you, Megan. I'd defend you against my own people so do you believe for a second that I'd just allow one of them to harm you?"

"Who's going to protect you?" She frowned at him.

That question obviously stunned him. "You doubt my fighting skills and strength? I'm cyborg, Megan. I'm stronger and faster than your human males."

She hesitated, biting her lower lip, and then released it. "Don't take this the wrong way," she warned softly. "But you're…" She shut up, not able to say it aloud.

"I'm what?" He stepped forward, his hands gripped her hips as he pulled her against him, their bodies flush against each other. "What am I?"

Megan had to clear her throat of the lump that formed there. "They appear human but they aren't. You're…" She hesitated.

"I'm what?" His voice deepened.

"Oh hell," she sighed, holding onto his arms. "You're outdated technology, Ice. You're sexy, hot, muscular, and kick ass but these Markus Models, they are advanced technology, cutting edge, and in a fight I think you'd lose. I don't doubt how strong you are or how good of a fighter but these things are…really bad news."

Ice's eyebrows shot up.

"They heal really fast," she said quickly. "Within minutes. It's that new rejuvenating artificial skin they have. They don't have bones, they have lightweight metals, and they are shielded. You shoot one of them in the head, which would normally take anything out, and they are going to get up. I saw some of the tests run on them to demonstrate how tough they were to investors. One of them walked through fire. It burned off his skin and he just kept going."

His hands rubbed her hips. "You're worried about me?"

"Yes. I'm worried about all of us. You, me, everyone on this ship and the *Star* you keep mentioning. I can't stress enough how unstable the Markus Models are or how hard they would be to kill. You're mostly flesh and blood. These things are androids with cloned flesh. They may appear more human than you do with your gray skin tone but trust me, they are machines."

"Maybe they didn't fix their electrical flaw so they will have a weakness in their design."

"The company wouldn't have unleashed them without fixing that."

Ice sighed. "The council has spoken and I made the deal with them that you'd help evaluate these things. It's going to happen. Perhaps they fixed the instability problems with them before they were put out by your company."

"I doubt it since they are refusing to return the bots and are looking to hook up with cyborgs instead. That sure wasn't in their programming so what else is wrong with them?"

"Earth Government thought we were flawed and wanted us exterminated. They were wrong, Megan. Perhaps you're wrong."

"I really hope I am but I don't think so, Ice." She leaned in and let her forehead rest against his chest. "I'm worried and scared."

His hands slid around her, hugging her tightly to his body. "I will protect you."

But who is going to protect you? She thought it but didn't say again. He thought he could handle anything but she doubted he'd ever gone against anything as scary as defense androids. Cyborgs had left Earth a long time ago and things had changed.

"I came to change my uniform. I have a vid conference with the council." He eased his hold. "I'll return to you afterward. We'll talk more then."

Megan nodded against his chest and looked up at him. "Okay." She didn't want to let him go but she released him as she stepped back.

Ice quickly changed his pants, then donned a shirt, and put on his boots again. He gave her a lingering look before he left his quarters. He didn't touch the pad and she realized he must be keeping his link to the ship active so he could remote control the doors.

Turning, she sank onto the bed, worried. A shiver ran down her spine. Ice had no idea what they were about to deal with but she had a pretty good idea this meeting wasn't going to go well.

She started to think, trying to remember everything about the Markus Models that she'd been told or heard rumors about while she'd worked at the testing facility.

* * * * *

"What is wrong?" Onyx stopped at the table and sat. "I've been watching you for five minutes and you didn't even notice when I entered the room."

Ice locked gazes with his friend. "The council ordered me to either hand Megan over since I refuse to kill her myself or I can form a family unit with her."

"So you're joining a family unit? I understand your grimness. We're of the same mind on that issue but she is human. There are advantages to taking one as your female. She will be ordered to stay at your side since she won't be trusted by other cyborgs. You'll have constant access to her and you do not have to share her body with other males. I am surprised they offered to allow that, considering our status. We've both overbred so our DNA is no longer required."

"I also informed them she is an expert on the Markus Models to make her valuable to them. We will be meeting their shuttle when the *Star* does, to bring Megan to that meeting."

Shock widened Onyx's eyes. "You did what? Why would you do that? Even I saw her terror when she spoke of them. She is convinced they are dangerous. I thought you wanted to protect her. If they are as unstable as she suggested then you are putting her at high risk."

"She is definitely at risk with the council. They reversed the order to have her killed since they have a use for her now. It wasn't a hardship to agree to form a family unit with her so they believe she feels loyalty to me."

"You have emotions for her."

"I do." Ice took a sip of his drink and ignored his food tray. "It angered me when I saw her distress after I informed her of the conditions for the reversal of their order. I believed she was upset at joining a family unit with me but instead her fear stems from meeting that enemy shuttle."

"So she agreed to the family unit arrangement?"

Ice hesitated. "I didn't ask her. I said I informed her. As a human I do not need her permission since on Garden they are considered property."

"Did you inform her of this?"

"No. I am not without intelligence."

Onyx grinned. "Your limbs are intact and I don't see any visible damage. Human women must be very different from our females. If you'd informed one of them of that fact they would have attacked you."

"Megan is nothing similar to our females in that regard."

"However she is, it obviously instills great faith in you since you're willing to put so much trust in her. You know she could use these defense models to attack us."

"She wouldn't do that." Ice glared at his friend. "I...trust her." It amazed him as that truth struck him but saying it aloud made him come to terms with it. "I really do trust her, Onyx. She's honest with me and she is worried about my safety over her own."

"I'm willing to rely on your judgment even if I do think you've been compromised by her influence. I'd trust you over anyone else I've ever known in my life. I'll inform the men and we'll ready for that meeting. I assume you want me to secure all information so they can't hack into our systems."

"Yes. You know what to do."

"Of course." Onyx nodded. "Go spend time with your female and I'll take care of everything."

Ice stood. "Thank you."

"I believe some things are worth keeping. I personally wouldn't hook up with a human but she's not in my bed so I can't imagine what it would be like to lose her."

"She really matters to me."

"Then do what you must to keep her. If that means we're facing danger when we go to that meeting then at least it will be an interesting day. It was getting a little boring around here now that we no longer have use of the sex bots. Some of the males are feeling a little sexual frustration after adjusting to regular pleasure. If it comes to a fight, it may be to our advantage. There is nothing worse than a testy male."

Ice disposed of his untouched food and walked through the ship. He had a lot to consider. He finally returned to his room and to Megan. He'd come to a decision.

* * * * *

Ice appeared tired and grim when he walked into his quarters. Megan stopped pacing and stared at him. She took a deep breath.

"I thought about this family unit thing while you were gone. This council of yours needs me and I'm willing to face my deepest fears to interact with the Markus Models for them but I won't allow you to be forced into marrying me against your will. Have them touch me so they

174

know I'm not lying and I'll tell them I'm on your side. It's the truth and I'd never want any of your people hurt. They'll believe me then, right? Do they have that lie detector ability the way you do?"

Ice paused inside the door and then walked slowly toward her. "They could do that."

"I don't want you forced into something you don't want to do just to save me, Ice. I don't want you unhappy or miserable. I really don't want you to grow to hate and resent me."

He paused, studying her. "You've been thinking of ways to circumvent a family unit with me out of a belief that I object to joining into a contract with you?"

"I know you don't want to get attached. You kept me in your quarters on the condition that didn't happen and now they are forcing you to be locked to me, right? I don't want to hurt you in any way."

Something in his eyes softened. "What about your emotions on the matter? What are your thoughts of forming a family unit with me?"

She hesitated, surprised that he'd asked her what she felt and thought. "Um...I wouldn't be opposed but not at the price it would cost you."

"It wouldn't cost me, Megan. We already share quarters and it's an arrangement that is working for both of us. I agreed to the council's terms and refuse to negotiate with them again for you. I made an ideal bargain with them."

"But—"

He cut her off. "That's it, Megan. It's done. I filed the paperwork and transmitted it. I'm just waiting for the official filing on Garden. We're contracted in a family unit."

"But you don't want to be tied down. You don't want—"

Ice closed the distance and grabbed Megan, jerking her against him to stare into her stunned gaze. "I want you."

She stared up into those beautiful silvery-blue eyes and saw raw emotion shining there. It hit her like a brick as she identified the look he gave her. Her heart raced and her hands reached up to grip his shoulders as she inched up on tiptoe to get closer to his face, to make sure she was seeing right.

The truth hit her then. "You love me, don't you?"

Ice's gaze drifted from hers, darting around the room, focusing anywhere but on her. Megan leaned closer into him, her hands sliding up his neck until she cupped his face. She had to blink back tears. He didn't deny it.

"Ice?" she whispered. "Look at me, please?"

He sighed and glanced down. "Yes."

"Yes, you're looking at me or yes, you love me?"

He attempted to turn his face away but Megan's hold on him tightened. He didn't struggle or shove her away. He just refused to look at her again, staring at the cleaning unit across the room instead. She took a deep breath, seeing a darker-gray color spread across his cheekbones as she studied his handsome face. He was embarrassed and then she understood.

"I love you, Ice." She whispered the words to him. "I think I've loved you since the moment you showed up on my screen when you walked aboard the *Folion*."

That got him to look at her, their gazes meeting and holding. She nodded at him. "Really. I love you and if you feel that way about me, I'd be thrilled."

He blew out air from his lungs and frowned. "I am not thrilled."

"But you love me, don't you?" She tried to hide her smile but failed when the grin wouldn't be denied.

"I do but you don't need to appear so gleeful over my weakness."

That killed her smile. "It's not a weakness. It's wonderful and the most precious gift you can share with someone."

His expression and gaze softened, along with his tone of voice. "A gift?"

"Oh yeah." She nodded vigorously. "Definitely a gift, Ice." She grinned again. "We need to celebrate."

"Why?"

"It's not the why you should be curious about but the how."

His eyebrow arched. "I don't understand."

Her grin widened. "We're going to get naked and have lots of sex."

He finally smiled back at her. "A human custom?"

"Oh yeah. There are some great things about humans."

His hands gripped her ass. "I have to agree."

Chapter Eleven

Fear had a taste and Megan didn't enjoying it one bit as she swallowed it down. The uniform Ice had put her in was black leather, similar to his own, only this one fit her smaller frame. It had been specially made for her. She stood still, attempting to ignore the heavy, uncomfortable weight of the shirt as they docked with the *Star*.

Ice's hand brushed her hip and she looked up at him. "You appear frightened. Hide your expressions."

"I'm not you. I don't have your control but I'll try."

He nodded. "Just stay at my side and if trouble breaks out get behind me and return to the *Rally*. I'll cover your exit."

That's what she feared most. Ice would end up fighting the Markus Models if something went wrong. The bump when they connected to the other ship was slight and it took everything inside Megan to move forward when the docking doors opened. Nervousness over boarding a large A-class ship full of cyborgs made her heart pound but Ice tugged her forward.

Cyborgs weren't a threat to her any longer, according to Ice, and she believed him. As they walked into a large cargo bay she nearly stumbled as dozens of cyborgs waited, all shades of gray skin tones, wearing black leather uniforms matching Ice's. A dark-haired one moved forward, smiling, and held out his hand to Ice.

Ice didn't just shake the other cyborg's hand but instead embraced the man. "Flint, it's good to see you."

"It's good to see you as well. I miss your daily humor." They released each other and the cyborg, Flint, turned his attention on Megan. He ran his gaze down her and then back up to her face, a dark eyebrow arching before he grinned at Ice. "What happened to you swearing you'd never trust a human woman sleeping in your bed?"

Ice backed up. "I hadn't met the right one yet. I thought you'd lost your senses when I took yours from that shuttle we boarded."

Flint chuckled. "She's our expert?"

Ice turned and, with a jerk of his head, motioned Megan forward. "Megan, this is my good friend, Flint. You'll get to know him when we do more joint missions in the future. The *Star* and the *Rally* usually travel together. I had taken the *Rally* crew for a short vacation when *Folion* was destroyed. Once that happened we were forbidden to return until you were assessed."

She took a step closer and thrust out her hand. "It's nice to meet you, Flint." She met his gaze as he took her hand, giving it a gentle shake, before releasing her quickly.

"You as well. I read everything Ice wrote in his report about what information you shared about these defense hybrids. Have you come up with a reason for why they would contact us? How much danger is my ship in?"

"They are dangerous, unstable, and I'll say it again. This is a mistake. You can't trust them. They are more advanced than anything you've ever come into contact with. It's been a long time since you were created and technology has changed drastically on Earth." She paused, glancing at Ice to see his frown, but turned her attention back on the cyborg who obviously commanded the bigger ship. "They are organic on the outside but under their cloned skin they are a classified metal that is near impossible to destroy. They can hack your computer systems, take whatever information they want, and probably even take control of your ship. They appear human but don't let that fool you. They are androids. Machines. They aren't similar to you in any way except they were created in part inside a cloning lab."

Flint stared at her, studying her face, and then sighed, giving his full attention to Ice. "A few members of the council arrived just before you did." He paused. "We're being graced with Councilman Zorus' presence." The large cyborg's voice deepened when he said the name. "He demanded to be present and speak to them himself. He is insistent that we can broker a deal and is rambling on about how useful an ally they will be."

"Damn." Ice was irritated. "Nothing good happens when he is around."

"Exactly." Flint gave a nod. "I have Mira locked in our room where she's out of sight and I put a few guards outside my quarters. I don't trust that bastard since he hates all humans." He focused on Megan. "My wife would like to meet you, Megan. Mira is from Earth. I'm afraid she may want to spend hours talking to you. I believe she's lonely for another woman to spend time with and I hope you will humor her."

A human had married the big cyborg? It surprised her but she managed a nod. "That sounds nice."

"Good." Flint turned, addressing the rows of cyborgs standing at attention. "I want everyone prepared for the worst. You heard Ice's female and read the report." He turned then, staring down at Megan. "If this goes bad, do you have any suggestions? We're prepared to attempt electrocution in case that flaw design wasn't fixed."

"Pray," she said softly.

The dark-haired cyborg softly cursed. "Great." He lifted his head, stared up at a camera, and nodded. "They are docking." He faced another door. "We're boarding their shuttle. If a fight takes place we are going to retreat and attack their ship. That is a target we know how to deal with."

Ice nodded and spoke softly. "You heard Flint. Keep linked to me and if this goes bad undock and we'll meet up at our preplanned destination. Do not wait for us to return. We'll stay aboard the *Star*." He met Megan's raised eyebrow. "I'm talking to the *Rally*. We're in constant communication."

Doors opened and Megan tensed, expecting the Markus Models to enter the large cargo bay but instead she saw four cyborg males approaching but they weren't wearing black uniforms. Instead they wore red matching ones. Ice tensed.

"The council," he whispered loud enough for Megan to hear. "Zorus is the one on the far left."

It stunned her that such a handsome man had such a black heart. He looked tall, probably at least six foot four with dark-brown hair tied back in a tight ponytail. He had thick, dark eyelashes that windowed a pair of sexy, dark-brown eyes that locked on her. The rage she saw when their gazes met had her inching closer to Ice as the four council members drew near. All cyborgs were beefy, strong men, but Zorus seemed particularly thick muscled in his shoulders and upper arms.

"Ice." Zorus glared at Megan. "That is what you risked your career on? She's not even attractive."

Ice moved suddenly, putting his body in front of Megan, blocking her view of the rude bastard who'd just insulted her. She knew Ice put himself between her and the council members to protect her.

"Councilman Zorus." Ice's tone turned chilly. "She's attractive. It's your perspective of humans that is disagreeable."

"They can't be trusted."

Flint cleared his throat. "The shuttle has docked with us and the Markus Models are waiting." Something in his dark eyes flashed. "Why don't you go first since you set up this meeting, Councilman Zorus?" He waved his hand toward another door. "After you, sir."

Megan craned her head a little to peer around Ice and watched as Zorus shot Flint a glare but he nodded. "They are going to be an ally against the enemy."

That had to be humans, Megan surmised. She stood there until Ice reached back, offering her his arm. Her fingers gratefully curled around his forearm as he led her to follow the four councilmen toward the waiting shuttle that held her biggest fear. The doors opened and the cyborgs entered in pairs, with Zorus at the lead.

For some reason the councilmen stopped quickly inside and Megan thought she heard one of them utter a harsh curse. They moved forward again and Ice's arm tensed under her fingers. She heard him mutter a four letter word and her gaze flew up to his. He stared at something ahead of them to the left. She had tall men blocking her view and didn't see what captured their attention until they were almost in the center of the small cargo hold.

Megan stared in horror at the far wall. One of the sex bots was naked, bound by her wrists pulled above her head, dangling a few feet from the floor, and her hair was gone. The now-bald bot blinked and as she turned her head to track the movement in the room, Megan got to see the back of its head from a side view. The rear plate of her skull was missing so her inner electronics were exposed. The bot's lips moved but no sound came out. At that point Megan saw the other damage that had been done to the bot. Her artificial skin had been cut open in places on her thighs and down one side by her hip to expose her inner metal frame.

"Oh my God," Megan gasped. "What did they do to her?" She took a step toward the bot but Ice's hand clamped down on her fingers, locking her to him, and kept her in place.

"Quiet," he whispered. "Mask your expressions now. They come."

She heard them before she could see them enter the room. She'd forgotten how heavy the Markus Models were with their metal interior frames and the resulting thumps their feet made on the cargo flooring as they drew closer. She had to inch away from Ice a little to see around the cyborgs in front of her but she couldn't go far since Ice had her hand pinned on his arm with his fingers gripping her. Four androids walked into the cargo area single file and then lined up side by side to face their visitors.

"Eerie," a cyborg muttered behind Megan.

She knew what he meant. The androids were exact replicas made from the same mold. If that wasn't bad enough, they moved in synchronicity, each movement a mirror as they silently studied the four cyborg council members. Their heads turned at the same angles, their gazes locking on each male one at a time, and finally someone spoke.

The councilman stepped forward a few feet and halted. "I'm Zorus. You requested asylum and we're here to discuss the terms." He glanced at the four artificially made men. "Are there more than four of you? Who is in charge?"

"We all are in command," they said in unison. "This is the number of our strength."

"Shit," another cyborg whispered from behind Megan. "So much for Zorus thinking there are a bunch of models willing to stand up to Earth Government. I'm glad there's not more of them. It's creepy the way they talk together."

Megan understood that sentiment as well and the uneasiness his voice revealed. The defense hybrids were hive minded, obviously linked together, and working as one unit. They hadn't been designed that way so it was something Megan surmised they'd changed in their own programming. She had a feeling that the council members were wishing they'd heeded her warning now as she watched Zorus take a step back from his potential new allies. He cleared his throat but before he could speak again, they did.

"You brought programmer Megan Bellus with you. As one of our terms, we demand the threat destroyed."

Ice reacted first, before Megan's stunned mind could translate that the machines wanted her killed. He released her and a heartbeat later put his body directly in front of hers. His hand reached for the weapon holstered to his belt and gripped it. A tall cyborg, a bald one, suddenly brushed against Megan's arm, stepping forward to her side. Ice turned his head, met the cyborg's gaze, and nodded.

"Get her out of here if this turns bad, Coal," he whispered.

The big, bald cyborg nodded grimly and whispered back, "I'll protect your female with my life."

Ice faced forward and moved to the right, putting himself in full view of the Markus Models. "We're not going to kill Megan Bellus for you. Why would you ask that of us? She's my wife and she's not a threat. We brought her with us because she's familiar with your kind. We wanted her expertise in our negotiations with you."

The four Markus Models locked their chilly gazes on Ice. "Humans are expendable, a threat to our existence, illogical, and we want her destroyed."

Coal reached out, his arm going across Megan's chest, and he gently pushed her behind him. He reached for his weapon as well, gripped it by the handle but didn't withdraw it from the holster. He backed up a step and Megan moved with him, having no other choice as the big cyborg pressed against her.

"I don't trust humans myself." Zorus stated. "She did form a family unit with a cyborg though, which makes her part of our society."

"We want the threat destroyed," the models demanded.

Megan inched over a little to peer between the cyborgs in front of her. She saw Zorus as he glanced back at her, their gazes meeting, and she saw his grim, suspicious look before he faced the Markus Models again.

"Why is she a threat to you?"

They refused to answer. Megan's mind went into overdrive. Why were they considering her such a threat? She'd worked with them but besides that, the only way she could possibly hurt them was if she used her programming codes but those had to have been changed. It was standard policy to do that as well as fix the flaws when a product was released from the testing stage for future use. Their codes would have changed unless... *Oh shit*, she thought.

"Ice?" she whispered. She wished she were linked to him mentally the way some of his men were so she could talk to him without the risk of being overheard.

Onyx moved to stand on the other side of her and leaned down. He pressed his lips to her ear. "What? Tell me and he can hear you. He doesn't want to move from his position."

Megan had to put her hand on his shoulder to lean in, nearly touching his ear with her lips. "I don't think Barcarintellus put them into production."

Onyx frowned, turning his head to stare at her.

She tugged on him, bringing his ear down to whisper into it again. "I think they may have escaped instead. That's the only reason I'd be a threat. I know their weakness and their shutdown codes. If they weren't fixed, modified by the company, and cleared for duty, those wouldn't have been changed."

Onyx straightened and his expression hardened. He said nothing but she saw Ice nod ahead of them so he and Onyx were obviously silently communicating. Onyx hunched down a little and met her eyes. He mouthed his words.

"What is the shutdown code?"

She licked her lips, wetting them, and took his hand. She met his gaze. "Mercy," she mouthed back and looked down. She showed him four fingers, then two, then four, and then one. She looked up. Onyx nodded. He understood.

"We request asylum with you," the Markus Models stated loudly. "We wish to integrate with your society and live with your people." They paused. "How many cyborgs survived? We would like an exact number."

Warning bells were going off inside Megan. Why did they want that information? It was an odd request.

Zorus hesitated. "We'd rather not give that information out."

"It is a logical question," the Markus Models stated louder. "We need to know the exact numbers of surviving cyborgs and their exact location. We demand to know."

Megan moved forward. Onyx grabbed at her arm but she jerked away and walked to stand next to Ice. She stared at the models and saw that they noticed her movement as all four of them turned their heads to stare at her. Ice reached out and put his hand on her arm, gently tugging to pull her behind him. She jerked back, holding ground.

"Authorization beta-one-four-four-six. State your real mission. That's a direct order."

"What are you doing?" Zorus hissed. "How dare you interrup—"

"We are going to exchange cyborgs for cash reward and then buy more models to conform to our mission and save the rest of our brothers," the Markus Models stated.

Megan's heart nearly stopped as the shock tore through her. Her gaze jerked up to stare at Ice. "We have about fifty seconds before they aren't frozen by that command," she told everyone in the room.

"Shut them down," Ice barked.

Megan nodded. "Authorization mercy-four-two-four-one."

"They were setting a trap for us," Zorus gasped, astonished. "They wanted us to lead them to Garden and the rest of our people."

"Megan stated it was a bad idea to meet with them in the first place." Ice glared at the councilman. "I put that in my report but you discounted her opinion because she's human."

"I hate to break up the finger pointing," Megan said loudly, "but just because I shut them down doesn't mean they'll stay that way. I don't know what kind of modifications they made to themselves. They obviously somehow escaped the testing facility. Barcarintellus didn't change their authorization codes so that's where they came from."

"You shut them down." Flint spoke. "Doesn't that mean they will stay off until they are turned back on?"

"Not necessarily. They are unstable and were always messing with their own programming." Megan stared up at Ice. "I say we fry them just to be sure. Since the codes weren't changed, nor were their flaws, they are still vulnerable to electrocution."

188

"No." Zorus shook his head. "We could study them. We'll take them to the *Vontage* and use that ship to secure them while we bring a team of our best scientists from Garden to run tests."

Megan glared at the man. "Let me tell you something, sir—"

"Shut it up," Zorus yelled, glaring at Ice. "I do not speak to humans. Silence her."

"They escaped a high-security testing facility," Megan spoke louder, unwilling to be shut up by the rude cyborg. "They would have turned them off and the only way I can figure they may have escaped is by bypassing that command somehow. You can bet that the guards didn't just allow them to walk out the doors. They—"

"I'll permanently shut it up myself," Zorus snarled, taking steps toward Megan.

Ice grabbed her, pulled her out of the advancing cyborg's path, but then another cyborg moved in his way as well. Zorus was blocked from getting closer to her. Ice glanced down and shook his head at Megan, silently ordering to her not talk anymore. She sealed her lips and kept them together.

Flint glared at the councilman. "They are dangerous. They lured us here to find out our numbers and obviously planned to trick us into leading them to our home world. We should end the threat now."

"If we are destroying all threats to us then every human should be taken out as well." Zorus marched right up to Flint and glared at him. "I give the orders."

"A human, my Megan, just saved us from making a fatal mistake to our future," Ice snarled. "These Markus Models should be destroyed. You refused to listen to her advice before but you were wrong. If she thinks they pose a danger, we should listen to her."

"I give the orders," Zorus snapped. He looked away from Ice and glanced at a few of the cyborgs around him. "You, you, you, and you. Come with me. We're going to pilot this shuttle to the *Vontage*."

"Perhaps the human is correct." One of the council members spoke.

"I refuse to listen to one of them." Zorus turned and stormed toward the doors that led to the interior of the shuttle they were on. "We're not going to pass on an opportunity to study the technology that Earth has come up with to make them. They could be the next threat we face if Earth Government ever sends these things after us. I want to know their weaknesses."

Two of the council members nodded, following Zorus while one remained. He sighed, glancing at the men around him. "You heard him. I believe it is a possibility that we may face this threat in the future. We have a rare opportunity to study them."

They were making a big, stupid mistake, Megan thought. She glanced up at Ice, seeing the frustration on his face as he stared at Flint. Flint had a grim expression as he shrugged.

"You heard their orders." He paused. "We'll warn the *Vontage* crew what is coming their way. Steel will take every precaution." Flint focused on Megan. "Will you share all your information with us so if this goes bad they can at least attempt to neutralize the threat?"

"Of course." She turned and looked up at the sex bot still hanging. "Ice?"

"Yes, Megan?" He inched closer.

"Can you please get the bot down? Please? I can't stand to see her that way. I think I can fix what they did to her."

Ice glanced at Onyx.

Onyx nodded. "I'll cut it down and bring it aboard the *Rally*."

"Thank you," Megan whispered, looking away from the damaged bot. What had been done to it was horrible. She didn't know if she could fix it but she couldn't stand to see one that way. "What about the other bots?"

"Coal? Find the other eleven bots if they are still on the shuttle and transfer them to the *Rally* quickly please, before they undock this shuttle from the *Star*. I figure you have about half an hour while they assess if they booby-trapped the systems before attempting to take control of it."

"Of course." Coal headed toward the doors that the council and the four ordered cyborgs had gone through.

Ice shook his head. "Let's contact Steel now and warn him." He held out his arm to Megan. "He'll want to talk to you, Megan. He's going to want to know everything you can tell him about those things, in case they somehow reboot since they are going to be on his ship. He's a good friend of ours and he's also married to a human. He's going to be furious that not only is Zorus bringing danger aboard the *Vontage* but that he'd dare go there in the first place. Zorus once attempted to prevent Steel from forming a family unit with his female."

"I really don't like Zorus," she muttered, wrapping her fingers around Ice's arm, allowing him to lead her back to the *Star's* cargo bay.

He answered her by snorting. "No one likes him."

They were walking toward the *Rally's* docking door when a cyborg approached. Ice turned to face him and his body tensed. "Darius."

The cyborg's attention wandered leisurely over Megan's body. "Aren't you afraid you'll break something so weak?"

"No." Ice's silvery-blue gaze narrowed dangerously. "Aren't you afraid I'll break you for insulting the woman in my family unit?"

Megan glanced between Ice and the other cyborg, wondering what was going on. The dislike between them was evident. Ice tugged her closer to his body and put his arm around her.

"What do you want? Your father is aboard the Earth shuttle."

"I'm aware. He linked with me and ordered me to find you to give you orders. You turned off your link. Your female is ordered for duty to assist with his new project. He is expecting her on the Earth shuttle immediately so she's on hand if there is a problem."

"No," Ice snarled. His arm dropped from around Megan's waist and he stepped forward, going nose to nose with the other cyborg. "She's the female in a family unit and I do not give my permission for her to be assigned to a dangerous mission. Councilman Zorus has no right to do that."

Darius took a step back and his dark eyebrows rose. "My father assumed you'd take that stand. I am to remind you that your DNA is no longer needed on Garden, nor is your female's. We don't want to contaminate our gene pool with your contributions any longer." He

192

lowered his gaze, staring at Megan. "And she is just useless in general unless a male needs sexual release."

Ice took a threatening step toward the other cyborg and Megan saw rage on his features. She grabbed his arm to stop him from hitting the jerk. If Zorus was his father then Ice would probably get in trouble if he decked the rude cyborg.

"It's okay," she said quickly as Ice jerked his head to stare down at her. "He's the one not worth it."

Ice stepped back and glared at the cyborg. Darius smiled coldly. "My father wants her on the Earth shuttle now."

"I go with her."

Relief was instant for Megan. She didn't want to be on the same shuttle with the Markus Models without Ice.

Darius paused, obviously listening to a voice in his head. "My father said that is acceptable. Proceed now."

"We need clothes."

"He said now." Darius jerked his head and smiled coldly.

Ice glared at the other man and his hands fisted at his sides. Megan rubbed the arm she still gripped. She wasn't happy to be stuck in the heavy leather uniform for however long it would take to reach the *Vontage* but she was too grateful to still be with Ice to really allow it to bother her.

"What is his problem?" she whispered as they walked away.

Ice stopped walking and met her curious gaze. "He's a completely sterile male in my breeding pact. The drugs do not work on him. His female requested my DNA as her donor for his child and the one for herself. It was successful both times and then she called upon me for a third time. After each breeding session, she offered me a place in their family unit but I refused. She already has two males in the family unit and he did not like her wanting me to join their unit."

Cyborgs do get jealous, she thought. "I understand."

Ice nodded. "We do not get along. He is angry that three offspring in his family are all from my DNA."

"I got it."

Ice sighed. "Let's go. Councilman Zorus can be an ass when he's made to wait."

Chapter Twelve

The bot had been taken down and was no longer within sight when they returned to the cargo hold of the Earth shuttle. Megan was grateful she didn't have to see that view again. The Markus Models stood frozen where she'd shut them down, their eyelids closed the way they were mandated to do to protect their cloned-tissue eyes.

"If they aren't going to destroy them, then within a few days, they are going to need maintenance."

Ice stopped walking and stared down at her. "Recharged?"

She hesitated. "Their living tissue needs supplements as well as recharging their power sources." She really took a good look at the room around her and saw the name of the ship painted on one of the bulkhead beams.

"Oh crap!"

"What is it?" Ice frowned, his gaze following to where she stared.

"This is the *Nugget*."

"Is that supposed to have meaning for me?" He arched an eyebrow as he met her gaze.

"This is Victor Barcarin's luxury shuttle."

"Who is he?"

She bit her lip and then sighed. Cyborgs really were out of touch with Earth if they didn't know the name of one of the richest men on four planets.

"You know how I work for Barcarintellus? Victor is the Barcarin in that first half of the company's name. His partner is Roy Tellus. This ship was designed for him last year and it's probably the envy of every person who owns a shuttle."

Ice's disbelieving expression almost made Megan laugh, even under these tense circumstances, as she watched him carefully run his gaze around the cargo hold.

"It looks standard to me."

"How many shuttles have you ever heard of that boast the best of everything? Remember how fast you were told this shuttle came at us when they were after the bots? That's just an example. The news on Earth ran tons of stories about it when Victor Barcarin first took possession of this baby. No cost was spared. It can hold thirty people comfortably so he can have his full personal staff with him wherever he travels—that's ten more than standard and we're talking really nice quarters with fresh water baths and showers. The plating on this thing is supposed to be superior to anything on the market."

Ice still frowned.

"From what I heard, you could fly it through a meteor field and it won't even dent."

"That's impossible."

"That's what the news said."

"They lie."

Megan stared up at him, having to agree since she knew, according to everyone on Earth, that cyborgs were all supposed to be dead. That had to have been posted on the official news channels at least once for everyone to believe it.

"I wonder how they stole it." She stared at the still Markus Models. "They had to have escaped while Mr. Barcarin visited the testing facility."

"It doesn't matter."

That was true enough. They had escaped, stolen the *Nugget*, and for some reason had come after the bots. A horrible thought struck Megan. "I bet those things activated the thief modes on the bots, looking for Clara."

Ice had started to move again, tugging her toward the doors to the interior of the shuttle when he paused. "Clara was the main computer on the *Folion*, correct?"

"Yes. If they had gotten their hands on her they could have controlled a lot of the company's assets. They could have blackmailed them to hand over more Markus Models. I bet they were disappointed when they realized *Folion* had been destroyed and Clara with it."

"We must have been their backup plan." Disgust laced his tone. He told the two cyborgs standing guard by the interior doors, "Don't take your focus from them."

"We won't," one of them promised. "They are nothing similar to us."

Ice glanced at the four still models and nodded his agreement. "They escaped Earth somehow and Megan doesn't trust that they will remain powered down."

197

"Understood," the other cyborg said softly as his hand reached for his weapon and his fingers curled around it. "We will remain vigilant."

Ice touched the pad by the door and it opened. He got his first glimpse of luxury living as they entered the hallway. He paused, staring at the floor and then the tiled walls. His eyebrows rose.

"Is that carpet and stone?"

Megan nodded. "Yeah."

"It's a shuttle. It's illogical."

"I know. Check out the paintings too."

Ice uttered a curse. "Humans have no common sense."

She couldn't argue that point. Ice turned left. "Let's go find the council members. I want to have a word or two with Zorus."

"Don't. He's an ass and we both know he doesn't have any sense."

"Zorus has no right to order you here. You're my female in a family unit. It is forbidden to order a female on dangerous missions without the permission of her male or males."

"You heard his son. That was his son, right?"

"Yes." Anger laced his tone again. "Because our DNA is useless on Garden, he believes he can get away with not following our procedures."

"I don't want you to get in trouble over me, Ice."

He refused to glance at her as he led her down a few corridors. He did pause when they came to a pair of life-sized statues of naked women. Megan nearly laughed at his dismayed expression.

"It's considered art," she explained.

198

"It's a waste of space in an already narrow hallway. Where are their heads? Were they broken off?" He turned, looking around.

Megan laughed. "They are replicas of ancient Earth history, I believe. I hope they are replicas anyway. I'd hate to think they risked precious artifacts by putting them on a shuttle."

"Why couldn't they reproduce them with heads?"

She chuckled again. "I don't know."

"Damn illogical," Ice muttered, walking again.

They found the other cyborgs in the piloting section of the shuttle. Zorus had taken the captain's plush chair while the other three council members had taken the other station chairs. The two remaining cyborgs stood guard just inside the door. Ice nodded at them and released Megan when they entered the room.

"Finally." Zorus punched in a command on the pad in front of him. "We were waiting for you to board. The systems are all online and it wasn't protected against an attempt to take command of it." He shook his head. "Stupid."

The engines flared and the slight vibrations were noticeable even through the thick carpet on the floor. One of the cyborgs wearing red spoke softly. "Undocking with the *Star*. I'm programming in coordinates to rendezvous with the *Vontage* and will test the engine abilities on speed limitations."

"Good." Zorus spun and glared at Ice. "Take your female back to the cargo hold. She is to stay with those *things*."

"We're at least a full shift away from the *Vontage*. I refuse to have Megan hungry and uncomfortable for that length of time. As you are so fond of pointing out, she is not a cyborg."

"You are refusing my order?"

"She's here when both of us know you had no right to order her to be on this mission. Do you really want to push it?"

Some of the anger eased from the councilman's face. "Take her and get her out of my sight until she's needed. Go find her a bed and food." He turned away to face the screen that showed nothing but empty space. "Weak," he muttered.

I'd rather be weak than a total asshole, Megan thought, keeping that opinion to herself. Fury gripped Ice's features as he spun on his heel, gripped her arm gently, and led her back into the hallway.

"He goes too far."

"He's an ass, just like most bosses are." She shrugged. "I'm not hungry but I wouldn't mind finding a bed."

"Sleeping quarters logically should be on the deck below this one. Are you tired?"

They located a lift and stepped inside it. She grinned. "No. I just want to find a bed and some alone time with you."

Surprise flickered in his expression as he stared at her. "Sex? Now?"

"I have no idea when we're going to be alone again."

The lift doors opened and they stepped out into another hallway. Megan walked to the first door and touched the pad. It didn't open. Ice brushed her hand aside, placed his there, and closed his eyes.

"What are you doing?"

"Reading the last input codes." His eyes snapped open and he removed his hand, punched in five digits, and the door opened. He smiled, meeting her gaze. "Implants have their advantages."

"I wish I could do that. Do all cyborgs have them?"

"Yes." He paused. "I do know one who has nonfunctioning implants. Coal is the male who I asked to retrieve the bots. His were purposely damaged when he was enslaved and we were unable to fix them."

"Did that happen when he was on Earth before your people escaped?"

"It's a long story I'd rather not go into right now."

She looked away from him and stepped into the dark room. The second she moved a few feet inside the living quarters, automated lights came on and she stopped in her tracks, her mouth dropping open in astonishment.

Ice nearly walked into her but just bumped her back slightly as he took in the room. "What the…?"

"Now that's a bed." A huge four-poster monstrosity took up a lot of the living space in the room. Megan reached for the front of her shirt and unfastened it. "How do you wear this heavy material? I think my shoulders are going to hurt tomorrow."

"It's not the material but the lining that makes it so heavy. It has an enforced mesh sewn between the linings. I wanted you protected."

"That's so sweet." It touched her that he'd put her in protective gear. "Strip."

His eyebrows arched. "I give the orders, remember?"

She grinned. "Right. Okay. Order me to get naked then. Did you see that huge bed? Tell me to go climb on it and prepare to have hot sex with you."

"Megan?" He looked stunned.

"Fear makes me a little hyper and I was terrified. My heart is still pounding and I have all this energy." She removed the shirt, dropped it on the floor, and bent over to remove her boots and socks. "I want you."

When she straightened to unfasten the pants, she grinned at seeing Ice quickly removing his clothing. His boots were already off. She loved admiring his muscular chest as he revealed it. It was a sight she knew she'd never grow tired of.

"Get on the bed."

She spun around and threw herself on the mattress, rolling over a few times to reach the center of it. Ice got on the bed after her, naked and aroused. His hard cock pointed straight out. Ice's gaze slowly wandered over her body.

"Roll over on your hands and knees."

She didn't hesitate, following his command, knowing it was his favorite sexual position. Ice bent over her, his cock brushing against her thigh, and one of his hands flattened on the bed to hold his weight up over her as his other hand reached around her hip and slid between her slightly parted thighs.

"Wider."

She understood and spread her legs farther apart. Just the sight of Ice naked did things to her so she wasn't surprised to be already wet when his fingertips found her as he rubbed against her slit and then spread it upward to her clit. Megan's head fell forward as a soft moan passed her lips.

"I love you touching me."

"You are so responsive." His voice deepened. "I love to touch you and hear the sounds you make."

"I love the way you play with me." She didn't miss their use of the "L" word. It warmed her inside that he'd even use it. "I love a lot of things about you."

He chuckled, his fingertip making slow circles around her clit that had her vaginal walls clenching and her biting her lip. The bed shifted a little as Ice moved, centering his hips to align with the curve of her ass. His hot, hard cock brushed the inside of her thigh and he stopped playing with her clit to grip his erection and guide it. A soft moan tore from Megan as he pressed against her, entering her slowly, stretching the inner walls of her pussy with the thickness of his shaft.

"So hot," he groaned.

"Touch me again, please?"

He sank into her deeper and released the base of his cock. His fingertip returned to her clit, pressing on it with just enough pressure to feel really

203

good. Ice withdrew a little and then his hips started to slowly rock as his finger slid up and down on her sensitive, swollen bud.

"Yes," Megan moaned. She lowered her upper body, bracing on the bed with her lower arms and elbows, and her forehead rested against the bed. "Don't stop."

"I won't."

He increased the pace, driving into her deeper and harder. The sensation of the thick crown of his cock rubbing against her cervix had Megan experiencing pure ecstasy. Her fingers clawed at the silky bedspread.

"Yes, yes, yes," she chanted.

His finger rubbed her clit faster as he pounded his hips against her ass, driving harder into her, and Megan's breath caught. She was going to come. Her muscles tensed, the feeling of Ice's cock fighting her tightness, making the pleasure more intense, and his hand lifted from the bed as he straightened, gripped her hip and he fucked her harder, faster, deeper.

"Ice!" Rapture tore through her as she started to climax. Her muscles twitched as she screamed into the bed.

"I've got you," he groaned and started to come hard inside her as his body jerked with each jet of his release that bathed her inside with spreading warmth as his movements slowed until he stopped.

They were both panting and Ice moved his finger away from her clit, sliding his palm higher on her stomach as he came down on top of her again, pinning her bent form under his. The hand on her hip moved and he hugged her around her waist, locking their bodies together.

204

"I could easily get addicted to you."

Megan smiled. *I'm already addicted to you*, she thought.

Ice, still buried deep in her body, nuzzled her head with his and rubbed her stomach. She could feel his cock throbbing like a heartbeat and her smile widened when he said, "Let me catch my breath and we'll go again. That just took the edge off."

"Sounds like a great plan to me. I want to be on top next time."

"If I allow it."

She laughed. "I'm betting I could—"

A loud siren sounded, blasting through the room. It startled Megan enough that she would have probably fallen over onto her side if Ice hadn't been wrapped around her, holding her in place. His entire body tensed and he swiftly pulled out of her body, rolling off her, and the bed.

"What is that?" Megan sat back, sitting on her legs, and put her hands over her ears. The piercing sound hurt her ears and she had to yell to be heard.

"I don't know," he yelled, bending down to grab his clothes. "Get dressed now. Hurry!"

She wiggled toward the edge of the bed, not wanting to move her hands from her ears. The sound deafened and a red light flashed by the door. Whatever had triggered the alarm was a mystery.

Ice put his pants on but not his shirt. He strode to the door, slapped his hand on the pad, and closed his eyes. She watched him as she released one ear, reached down and found her shirt. Ice released the door and spun. The look on his face told her the news wasn't good.

"Those damn human look-alike robots rebooted," he roared. "Move it!"

Terror slammed through Megan so hard her knees buckled and she fell back onto the edge of the bed, gaping at Ice. Her worst nightmare had come true. The damn things had gotten around their programming and she had no further doubt in her mind that was how they'd escaped the testing facility on Earth. No one had thought they could do that since they weren't supposed to be able to bypass a shutdown code. She'd been afraid they could but hadn't really wanted to believe it was possible.

"Get dressed. They are attacking the guards, one of whom is severely injured. We need to get to Control and help take them out."

She bent, her hands shaking, as she reached for her pants. She fumbled but got her legs into them. Standing proved trickier since she still shook badly. Ice suddenly moved in front of her, his boots on already, and helped her yank her shirt on. She only did a few of the snaps, leaving the lower buttons over her stomach undone.

Ice gripped her hand and ran for the door, dragging her more than leading her since her legs didn't want to work right. She knew that Ice thought they could win in a fight against the androids but he hadn't watched the things walk through walls of fire and not even flinch as their cloned skin completely burned away. They experienced no pain, no emotions, and they were killing machines. She vaguely realized she was barefoot but she didn't argue the point as Ice forced her into the hallway, one hand gripping her, his other hand withdrawing his weapon from the belt he'd snapped on when he'd dressed.

The alarm fell silent as they reached the lift. Ice froze and Megan did too. She stared up at him with raw fear. "What does that mean?"

"I don't know. I can't link to the other cyborgs on this ship without touching access panels first to hold the communications open. I didn't hack their computer to gain remote access." His voice turned harsh. "I was too focused on fucking you instead of acting rationally."

Her mouth opened, not sure what to say to that, but the lift opened at that moment. Ice pushed her forward into it, steered her into the corner, and released her. He spun around, faced the doors, and touched the control. The doors closed and then he stepped back, pinning her to the wall, and pointed his weapon at the doors.

"If they are out there, I want you behind me so I take their weapon fire instead of you. I'll attempt to close the doors and get you to another floor. Run and hide. Take my weapon if I don't survive."

Ice was willing to die to protect her, using his body as a shield, and it brought tears to her eyes as love for him swelled painfully in her chest. She started to pray for his safety. If anything happened to Ice...she couldn't even imagine life without him now. The lift moved and she held her breath, her heart hammering when the lift stopped and the doors opened. She couldn't see what waited in the corridor, if anyone was there, but then Ice took a step forward.

"Stay on my heels."

She moved, breathless as she tried to keep up with Ice, whose long legs and strength gave him such advantage. The hallway was clear and he stopped at the curve so fast she ended up slamming into his back. He growled something low but she didn't catch what he said. He hesitated, peered around the corner and then started moving again. They were nearing the control room when the doors ahead to the left opened.

Ice's reflexes where fast as he threw himself against the wall, his weapon aiming at the open door, while his other arm shot out to slam into Megan. She hit the wall hard beside him. It knocked the breath from her lungs, and she found herself pinned where Ice held her. She gasped in air and turned her head, only able to see Ice since he'd put his body between her and the threat again.

"Both of them are dead," Councilman Zorus' voice called out. "We need to get to the emergency pods."

"What pods?" Ice released his hold on Megan and stepped away from the wall. His weapon lowered. "It's a shuttle. There was no pod in the cargo hold. What is the status on the androids?"

"They killed our men guarding them but before Vess died he blew out the power to the doors. The Markus Models are currently trapped inside the cargo hold but it won't keep them for long. They are using a cutting tool to burn through the bulkhead." Zorus had turned a sickly pale gray and fear showed in his eyes as he stared at Ice. "We discovered six life pods onboard when we pulled up the designs to see if we could open the exterior cargo doors or separate that area safely from the rest of the shuttle if we sealed the bulkheads. They are located on the same floor as the living quarters."

"This shuttle isn't big enough to hold a pod anywhere but in the cargo hold and definitely not that many." Ice wasn't convinced. "Are you sure?"

"It's in the shuttle schematics," Zorus snapped. "Move. We don't want to stay here."

One of the cyborg council members nodded. "We set a fire in Control so they can't use the shuttle to come after us and Mellno is sealing the bulkheads between us and the cargo hold to slow their progress in reaching us before we can escape. He'll be along shortly."

Megan realized that one of the two cyborg guards was gone, only one remained with the four council members. Ice spun and gripped Megan's upper arm. Moving fast, he yanked her along the corridor back to the lift.

The seven of them were cramped in the lift. Ice kept her against his body. She looked up at him, saw the grim set of his jaw, and knew her fears were justified. They were in really deep shit.

The doors opened and they rushed down the hallway to a curve. One of the council members stopped, frowning, and examined the wall. "I don't understand. There should be doors here for the pods."

Megan inched away from Ice's body, fighting his tight hold, and saw six squared, large wall tiles instead of doors. She'd seen them before once, in that vid about the shuttle, and had completely forgotten about them until that moment.

"Shit!"

"What is it?" Ice stared down at her.

"Let go."

He released her arm and she pushed past two of the council members, her hands touching the tiles. She found a button along the seam at the top and pushed it. The tile moved and she jumped back as it slid out from the wall, the cyborgs scrambling to get out of the way so they weren't crushed as it extended outward into the hallway.

"They are life capsules," Megan explained, staring at the long, box-shaped cylinder she'd revealed before lifting her gaze to Ice. "Each one only holds a single person."

Zorus broke the silence that met her explanation. "How do you open them?" He stood behind her, ending up on her side of the hallway where it had divided when the pod had blocked it.

Megan hesitated. "I don't know. I've never seen one in person, just in a vid, and they didn't exactly show how they worked. I just remember they were concealed in the wall and they are state-of-the-art."

"Move," Zorus pushed her roughly out of his way and touched the metal. A popping noise sounded and the lid started to lift.

Megan stared at the cushioned, black interior and shivered. It reminded her of a coffin, only much deeper than a burial one. On the interior of the lid were controls. Zorus softly cursed.

"We have no choice. Parlis, get in. You are first."

The councilman didn't look happy but he moved, climbed inside the box and stretched out flat. His big shoulders barely fit side to side but he had plenty of leg room. He nodded and then studied the panel above him.

A rumble sounded from somewhere in the ship and the lights flickered. Under Megan's bare feet she felt a vibration. Her gaze flew to Ice.

"Explosion," he told her softly. "I believe the Markus Models have left the cargo hold or the fire that was lit in Control is causing great damage."

The lid to the pod slowly shut, hissed loudly as it sealed, and the entire thing slid back into the wall. Megan backed up, bumping into the cyborg guard. After the square panel sealed against the wall, they heard the pod being expelled from the shuttle. It sounded as if it had been shot into space—a whooshing sound.

"He's clear." Zorus sighed. "I have short-range communications."

"How?" Ice frowned.

"It's a council upgrade," one of them explained softly, touching another panel and activating the pod to withdraw from the wall. "We need to communicate at times without words so we are able to link together."

Two of the council members climbed into activated pods, closed them, and they slid into the wall. Three pods remained.

Zorus visibly relaxed. "The three council members are clear and out of my range now but they made it. I wanted to make sure it was safe before I used one and it is. Now I will go." He tried to step around Ice.

"There are only six pods," the cyborg guard stated softly, his gaze locking with Ice's. "There are eight of us if Mellno is alive."

"We're council." Zorus glared at Ice. "Our lives are more important. Leave Mellno and the human behind. That's an order!"

Chapter Thirteen

Ice blocked Zorus' way to the three remaining capsules. "You expect me to leave my wife and one of our own men behind to die?" He grabbed the councilman and slammed him against the wall, growling in rage. "You did this by putting us in this dangerous situation. Megan warned you that those androids were unstable but you wouldn't listen. Your hatred for everything human has brought us to this moment."

"Release me. That's an order. I'm leaving. Kill him if your wife matters so much. I don't care who you save but let me go!"

Ice pinned the councilman tighter against the wall and turned his head, staring at the guard. "Go."

The cyborg hesitated.

"He told me to kill you, Roan. You heard him. Are you really going to protect him? Take the vessel and go." Ice stared at the other man.

The guard turned, activated the capsule that slid out from the wall, and quickly climbed in. He hit the button to seal the lid, his gaze locking with Ice's. "I owe you my life, Ice. I won't tell anyone what happened."

In other words, he wouldn't tell anyone that Ice had chosen to save his life over a council member. Ice turned his head the other way. His gaze locked with Megan's.

"Go, Megan. When you're safe I'll release him so he can use the last one."

Shock burned through her. "You're going to stay behind?"

212

"He's a council member. I may dislike him but I won't kill him."

"I'm not leaving you." Hot tears filled her eyes and she had to blink them back. "Those Markus Models will kill you or return you to Earth. Either way you'll die. No."

"Fine. Both of you stay. Release me. Those things are coming. I just heard the lift doors." Zorus struggled but couldn't break free of Ice's hold on him.

Ice spun, keeping one hand on Zorus and his other hand lifted, his weapon pointing toward the bend of the hallway. In seconds a large shape rounded the corner and Megan gasped. It wasn't a Markus Model or the other cyborg guard, Mellno. It was the bald cyborg. The one Ice had asked to get her bots. He was out of breath, had cuts on both arms, and a torn shirt.

Ice lowered his weapon. "Coal? What are you doing on board? You should be on the *Star*."'

"With my damaged implants I couldn't connect to the shuttle computer." He touched his head. "I couldn't bypass the doors that locked me inside a storage room when I entered it in search of the remaining bots. It seems some doors you may enter but need a code to exit. What is going on?"

"No time to explain."

Ice turned and his gaze locked with Megan's. She could see fear in his blue gaze. His voice rang with desperation when he spoke. "I love you, Megan. Get in the damn life capsule for me."

"No." She refused to leave him. "We'll fight them. We'll—"

213

A loud boom reverberated through the ship. The gravity stabilizers wavered so all four of them lost their balance and slowly lifted from the floor. The lights flickered and the gravity restored, slamming them to the deck.

"The shuttle is unstable," Zorus yelled. "Release me. I'm a council member. I'm giving you a direct order." He tried to shove Ice again.

Ice punched Zorus in the face, hard. The cyborg grunted and then went limp but Ice grabbed him with both hands, holding him up. He turned and stared at Coal.

"There are only two pods left and they only hold one person each."

Coal closed his eyes for a few seconds and then opened them. He lifted out his arms. "Give him to me. You both need to escape now. I'll stay behind."

Ice didn't move. "Coal, you and Megan are taking the life capsules. I'm staying behind with Zorus."

Coal shook his head. "You have a woman. I have no one, Ice." He hesitated, lifted his hand, and touched the back of his head. "I am damaged. I am no longer useful without active implants. You heard our doctors. The scar tissue is too severe to replace them. I couldn't even get myself out of a simple locked door without tearing through a wall with my body strength. Save your own life and be happy with your female."

"Please come with me," Megan begged. "Ice? I love you."

He turned his head, his beautiful silvery-blue gaze holding her captive with a sad look. "I have strong issues with tight spaces, Megan. I can't get into one of those capsules even if I were willing to allow Coal to take my

214

place by staying behind. I would do almost anything for you but I just can't put myself into that thing without losing control. I would damage the interior of the capsule when I struggled to get out of it, reasonable or not, and it would be a waste of two lives when one could be saved."

Megan blinked. "You're claustrophobic? Seriously? Is that what you're telling me?"

"Yes."

"But you're a big, strong cyborg." She knew her mouth was agape in astonishment. "Just shut off your emotion, do that thing you do and activate those chips you told me about. I know you said you like to feel everything but you can feel after we're safely away from this damn place."

"I was tortured," Ice admitted. "I know the fear is illogical but I'm unable to shut it down even when I've attempted it. It's too deeply instilled."

"But you—"

"I'm sorry," Ice said, cutting her off. "Coal, promise me you will protect her from the council. Don't allow them to harm Megan."

"I swear," Coal agreed. "Ice? Look at me."

Ice turned to face Coal and Megan watched in utter shock as the bald cyborg threw a powerful punch that landed directly on Ice's chin, sending the man she loved into an unmoving heap on the floor with the already unconscious Zorus. She was so surprised she couldn't even move for seconds. Her gaze lifted and Coal sighed, staring back at her. He shrugged.

"He can't be fearful if he's not conscious to experience emotion." He bent and grabbed Ice under his arms. "Open a pod. I'll place him inside it

215

and you take the remaining one. When he wakes, tell him to live a happy life for me, and that will make us even. I kept my promise. I protected your life since you won't be in any danger with a live male in your family unit."

She numbly moved and activated a pod. The smell of acid smoke teased her nose and she sniffed. Coal frowned and inhaled. He looked grim as their gazes met.

"The fire has spread inside the walls, into the electrical conduits is my best estimation. It's just a matter of time before the damage is so severe that no life will be sustainable. We don't have much time. Open it."

The pod had slid out fully from the wall and she touched the top, activating the lid to open up. Coal adjusted his hold on Ice's large body, cradling him in his massive arms enough to lift him over the edge and settle his body down. Megan only hesitated for a second before she climbed in after him. A hand grabbed her arm, stopping her. Her head jerked up.

"What are you doing? These are designed for one individual."

"If he wakes before we're picked up, he's going to freak out and may get himself killed. If I'm on top of him I can keep him calm and still." She paused. "And I'd rather risk both of our lives than just leave you behind to die."

Coal released her. "You're brave."

"Actually, I'm scared shitless. I don't want to die, but if I do, I'm with Ice. It's the only way I want to go out. Is it just me or does this thing look similar to a deep coffin?" She tried to joke, desperate to find some humor so she didn't start crying. "Talk about irony, considering I might die in it."

Coal smiled softly. "I'm going to put myself and the council male into the last pod so we at least have a chance of survival as well. Good luck, Megan. You're worthy of Ice. He's a good male that I am honored to call friend. Tell him that please."

"I promise. Thank you."

Megan lay facedown on top of Ice's limp body. Her thighs were flush with his and her cheek rested on his bare chest over his heart. She looked up to peer over her shoulder as Coal reached to activate the lid. She saw the release control when the lid sealed closed because it was the only thing that glowed. It turned red as the pod slid back into the wall and then it jerked to a stop. The light flashed to green. Her hands shook as she shifted enough to bend her arm up and over her shoulder. Her fingers brushed the button, pushed, and then she cried out in surprise.

The pod shot them away from the shuttle, the force suddenly sucking her tightly against Ice, obviously designed to do that to hold the occupant in place. The loud pod engines hummed as they burned strongly to send the capsule flying into space and away from the shuttle. Minutes passed before the engines suddenly died and an eerie silence settled around her, only broken by their breathing.

The gravity stabilized so she could move again as she lifted her head and stared into the utter darkness around her. It was pitch black, no lights were on the control panel above her any longer and she wondered if they were just going to remain trapped in space until they ran out of oxygen or until someone located the capsule. She really hoped that a cyborg ship was on its way, not sure if the council had a chance to make anyone aware of their predicament.

"Emergency life capsule activated." A female computer voice startled Megan. "I am currently triangulating our location and will make exact calculations to set a course to Earth. I will send distress signals for pickup of any Earth vessels we may come into contact with as soon as we are within transmission range of one. I currently am not showing any on radar."

"Delay that order," Megan gasped. The last thing they needed was to be piloted to Earth or to have the computer hail Earth ships to come pick them up. They'd rescue them all right but then turn Ice over to Earth Government.

"Unable to accept command. What is the abort code for auto programming?"

"Oh shit," Megan hissed. "Emergency response." She knew the universal code to take command of a computer.

"I am in emergency response mode."

"Abort auto programming."

"Unable to comply without authorization. I will dose you if you do not comply with auto procedure. The capsule is fully functional, my diagnostics read no damage and oxygen levels are acceptable."

We're in a world of shit, Megan though. The computer could dose them, which boiled down to the computer having the ability to release a gas with the oxygen it pumped in for her to breathe that would knock out an unruly, panicked passenger. Usually a captain of a pod would literally dose a freaked-out person with a shot but since it was a single capsule totally controlled by the onboard computer, gas made sense.

"I am calm," she lied.

"Understood. Location mapped." The computer paused. "We are nine days from Earth. I am setting course."

"Did your sensors read an extra passenger?" She hoped to confuse the computer and stall it. "Lights please."

A dim light filled the capsule interior, barely bright enough for Megan to get a good look at her surroundings. Above her were some controls but she didn't see the panel for the computer. She twisted her head and caught sight of it down by her feet. It had to be the access and she needed to get to it. She doubted she could hack the computer to take control of it but it was all she could think to do.

It had to be at her feet. She ground her teeth in frustration and tried to turn around. She realized quickly that she couldn't flip around. She wiggled and rolled over to face the top of the lid with her back against Ice's limp body. She attempted to sit up but she couldn't do more than lift up two feet before the lid blocked her. The heavy pants she wore hampered her movements.

"Two life forms confirmed," the computer stated. "That is against life-capsule specifications."

Megan immediately became awash with relief. "Perhaps you should run a complete analysis on possible ways to conserve resources to make sure both life forms survive the trip to Earth. I suggest you check with your manual."

"Running scenarios."

Megan wondered if she had minutes or hours before the computer stopped looping its programming, searching for a solution. She needed to figure out a way to make her body small enough to squeeze into a ball. She reached down, unfastened her pants, and shoved them down, kicking at the legs until they slid from her ankles, freeing her completely.

She took a deep breath, blew it out, and pulled her knees high up into her chest. She rolled onto her side, keeping in a tight formation, and tucked her head up, spreading her knees slightly to make room. She reached out with one arm, gripped a handful of Ice's pants, and started to pull. Her body moved, her ass rubbing against one side of the container while the back of her head pressed against the other side. She pulled harder, tucking her body tighter together. A slow inch at a time, she turned until she got her back clear of the side.

She had made it. She stretched her legs out, careful not to kick Ice in the face, and rolled onto her stomach. She reached up, grabbed Ice's leather-covered ankles, and pulled herself toward them and the panel just inches from the soles of his boots.

"Assessment made," the computer stated.

Megan wanted to curse. She'd hoped to confuse the computer for a while. "What is the conclusion?" Her fingernails explored the panel, trying to pry it off.

"I am adjusting oxygen levels to low. Passengers may experience lightheadedness if they move around but they will not suffocate. There is no reason to fear immediate death. I will cut food and liquid rations in half.

Passengers may experience hunger but each passenger will be permitted to have one nutrient bar every twelve hours and two ounces of liquid. It will be the bare minimum to sustain life."

The panel popped off and Megan stared inside, squinting at what she had to deal with. She mouthed a silent curse, studying the mass of wires and circuit boards.

"I'm reading an open panel."

"Yes, you are. One popped off. I'll put it back on," Megan lied.

She inched closer and read the tops of the integrated circuits. Each were labeled clearly with numbers but that didn't do her much good. Her expertise was in programming, not hardware, and she really doubted the computer would give her instructions on how to disable the navigational system or take the engines offline, if it were even possible to from that panel. Then again, she could give it a try.

"Computer, what kind of navigational system are you running? I'm worried about your accuracy."

"Unable to share that classified information."

"If you conserve energy by routing it to life support instead of navigation, will that increase power to life support?"

"Affirmative."

Hope soared in Megan. "On that basis, I am ordering you not to start engines and route all power to life support. Is it in your directive to override standard procedure to avoid risking human life?"

"Affirmative."

I've got you now, Megan thought. "I am ordering you to route all power to life support and keep the engines off."

The computer hesitated. "Is a human injured? According to my estimation it is possible to do both if I lower oxygen levels."

"I'm injured," Megan lied. "I need full oxygen levels. I'm having trouble breathing."

The low sound of a fan hummed to life and Megan relaxed, setting the panel back in place. The computer had responded to her commands. She'd found a loophole in its programming.

"Reserving all excess energy for life support. Navigational systems powered down, engines powered down. Scanning for possible rescue vessels and will emit a distress signal when one comes within range."

"Thank you." Megan closed her eyes and lowered her face, resting it on Ice's leather-clad lower leg. Her tense body relaxed. *That was close and I got lucky,* she thought.

Time passed as Megan lay there. Ice remained unconscious but it was a blessing. She knew she needed to move, needed to twist her body up and turn around again so she and Ice were facing the same way, but she admitted that she'd been through an ordeal. She worried that the Markus Models might be able to come after the life capsules. She also hoped that if a ship did find them, it belonged to cyborgs.

Ice twitched and softly groaned. Alarm rushed through Megan. She pushed up and twisted her head, watching him lift an arm, bump her foot, and then he touched his face.

"What the—"

"It's all right," Megan said quickly. "I'm with you and don't move."

The big body under her tensed, his muscles tightening, and she lifted up higher, bumping her head on the top of the lid, but watched as Ice lifted his head. She couldn't miss the stark, pale expression on his face as he realized where they were.

"I'm with you. Don't move, okay? It's tight in here and if you struggle you're going to hurt me."

His eyes were wide, alarmed, and the fear he experienced couldn't be denied as he locked gazes with her. His mouth opened and a soft moan came out. A new expression gripped his features, twisted them, and she knew panic when she saw it.

"Ice, listen to me. It's all right. I'm here, I'm with you, and we're really okay. Take a deep breath. There is plenty of air."

"What happened?" His tone deepened into a raspy, harsh sound before he started to pant. "How did I get in this thing?" His hands moved and he gripped her calves, his hold painful. "Megan, what did you do?"

"Coal did it actually. He hit you and knocked you out. He put you inside the capsule and I didn't want you to wake up alone so here I am." She forced a smile.

He stared at her, horrified. Megan bit her lip and tried to think of anything to say to calm him. She couldn't even promise him that rescue from his people would come soon.

"I'm with you and we're together. Just listen to my voice, okay?"

His fingers moved, rubbed her legs, and he dropped his head back as he closed his eyes tightly. "I need to get out of here." His breathing increased and his legs under her shifted, one heel digging into the soft floor.

She didn't see an emergency kit as she turned her head to search for one. The capsule didn't seem to contain one so the thought of knocking Ice out was a useless one. She needed to distract him and fast, before he totally lost it. She could tell he was about to with the way he shifted again, softly moaned, and his hands trembled where he gripped her legs.

She needed to turn around, get nose to nose with him, perhaps cup his face, make him stare into her eyes and get control of him. "Ice, I'm going to turn around, okay? You need to let go of my legs so I can curl into a ball again and wiggle enough to twist back to you."

He shook his head, his hold on her legs tightening instead of loosening. "I need to get out of here."

Shit, he is about to have a full-blown panic attack. He wouldn't release her so she bent her knees, spread her legs until she straddled his waist, and then wiggled back a little, hoping to force him to release her. The movement only changed his hold on her so her knees ended up under his armpits, his arms hooking just under her knees on her lower legs, and he turned his face into her skin, breathing hard against it.

She pushed up, getting on her hands and knees, her back brushing the top of the interior, and looked down. She hovered over his lap and couldn't figure out how to twist with him gripping her.

"Ice, you need to let me go so I can turn around to face you."

"I need to get out of here."

"Damn it, Ice." Frustration swelled inside her. "You're a big, warrior cyborg. You were willing to take on Markus Models without batting an eyelash but now you're being a baby about a little room issue?"

"I know it's unreasonable," he whispered. "It's not logical. It's…" He paused. "I'm not fighting. I want to hit something. I want to kick my way out. I am resisting the urge. Just talk to me."

Megan tilted her head, his lap drawing her attention, and her eyebrows rose. She couldn't miss the thick, long bulge trapped under his leather pants in an upward angle toward his waist. She surmised his fear had his blood surging throughout his body. An idea struck her.

"I'm going to distract you, Ice. Okay? I'm going to relax you."

"Talk to me."

"Do you know what I called you before I knew your name?"

"What?"

"Tall, gray, and sexy." She braced one hand, balancing her upper weight on it, and lifted the other, reaching for the fasteners of his pants. "I would lie in my bunk and fantasize about touching every inch of you. I wanted to know if you were as muscular as you looked on screen, run my fingernails down your back, and know what it would be like to have you inside me."

"What are you doing?" He sounded only slightly calmer and less panicked.

She opened his pants, shoving at them with one hand, and freed enough of his cock to gain access to most of it. The thick shaft was hard and sprang up as soon as she moved the leather out of the way.

"Megan? What—"

"Close your eyes for me. We're on your bed on the *Rally*."

She licked her lips and bent forward, her hand gripping his shaft. Ice hissed in surprise as Megan ran her tongue over the crown of his cock, licking him, and swirling a circle around the edge where crown met shaft.

"This isn't going to work." He softly groaned. "Your mouth is so hot."

"We're on your bed—imagine us there—and I'm going to do all kinds of wonderful things to you. Just relax and allow me to take care of you." She licked him again. "Just focus on me, on this."

Ice's breathing changed and his hips lifted a little. One arm released her leg and his hand wiggled between them to his hip and he shoved his pants lower. Megan smiled when more of his cock was freed and wrapped her mouth around Ice, sucking slowly on his aroused flesh.

"Megan." He groaned her name softly. "That feels so good. It's working."

She moaned, knowing he would feel slight vibrations from it. He hardened even more as she slowly moved up and down on him, turning her head at different angles, and then rose up until just the tip of his cock rested against her lower lip. She circled her tongue over it again.

His arm moved, releasing her other leg and his hands were suddenly shoving her shirt up her body so the bottom of it bunched on her lower back. His hands gripped her inner thighs and slid upward. He caressed her skin as she continued to slowly tease and taunt him. When his cock hardened so tightly that she knew he was about to come, she stopped sucking on him. Megan released him with her mouth.

"Help me turn around."

He hesitated and then his hold on her eased. "How? Why the hell did you lie opposite me?"

"I didn't start out this way. I'll explain it all to you later." *When we're out of this mess, if we survive*, she thought. "I have an idea. Spread your legs wide apart so they are against each side and then bend them up once I'm totally between your thighs."

He shifted his legs, spreading them, and Megan crawled forward a little. She had more space this way and curled into a ball, shifting onto her side, and wiggled until she turned around. She smiled and looked up at Ice as she got back on her hands and knees and started to move up his body until she had her hands next to his waist. He was totally fixed on her now, his focus changed from fear to getting off. Her plan had worked. Horny, seriously turned-on males, be they human or cyborg, had that in common.

"Close your legs now."

They shifted so her legs moved to the outside of his. She crawled up more, until she ended up face to face with him. She smiled and braced her weight on her bent knees and one hand then, reaching behind her, she gripped Ice's cock. She wiggled back, holding him in place and got him into position. She slowly sank down on his cock, moaning at the wonderful feel of how wet she was for him and how her body accepted him. She released her hold on his shaft and settled on him until he was fully seated inside her snug pussy.

"Perfect technique to alleviate my fear." He still appeared a little pale but the fearful, panicked look was gone from his features. "Just keep me occupied. If anyone can do that, it is you."

She chuckled. "I thought so. Now comes the best part." She lifted up then slammed down hard and fast.

Pleasure shot through her entire body at the fast motion and the way his thick, hard shaft rubbed her in all the best places. Nerve endings shot signals directly to her brain and she moaned Ice's name.

His hands gripped her hips and he lifted her easily before pulling her down on him fast. Megan threw her head back and lightly bumped the lid of the life capsule, reminding her that she needed to stay bent forward, no room to totally sit up on him in the confined space. She gripped the curve of his shoulders so she was stretched out above him.

"Slow," she urged. "We have time."

His eyes widened in a look of panic and Megan wanted to curse for reminding him with her thoughtless words that they were stuck out in dead space. She rolled her hips, her fingernails raked his skin, and she stared into his beautiful eyes. *Distract him quickly*, she ordered herself.

"I've been thinking." She rolled her hips again, teasing him, and keeping the sexual tension high. "If we're a family unit we should probably have a child at some point."

Ice's entire body tensed and he gripped her hips, locking her on top of him so she couldn't move. His head lifted and he frowned. The fear melted out of his gaze to be replaced by something akin to shock.

"A child?"

228

She nodded. "Not right off but I'm no longer opposed. You want one, whether you are willing to admit it or not. I saw your pain and longing when you talked about the ones on Garden that you created. As long as you swear you'll never leave me or divorce me, well, I'd be happy to have one with you. My biggest objection is because of my past."

His mouth hung open and he didn't say a word. Megan figured she'd stunned him speechless. He wasn't thinking about where they were, that was for sure. She licked her lips and tried to move on him but he kept her in place with his big, strong hands that gripped her hips.

"It's something for you to think about."

"You want me to do that now?" His eyebrows shot up.

"Sure."

"Megan." He frowned, causing grooves to appear at his mouth. "My DNA is considered overused and I'm no longer valued on Garden."

She slid down on him, going nose to nose with him until their breaths mingled. "I happen to think your DNA is priceless and a child with you would be the best gift ever when we're ready to have one. I love you, Ice. I never want to be without you and I'd be honored to give you little Ice babies."

"Babies?" His eyes widened. "Now you want more than one?"

She laughed at his expression and lowered her gaze to his mouth. "Kiss me. We can practice making them until we're both ready to discuss this again. You can tell me how many since I know you're a control freak."

Beautiful silvery-blue eyes narrowed and he suddenly drove his hips up, forcing his cock deeper inside her. "Was this mention of offspring just to keep me calm?"

A moan tore from her lips. She shook her head. "I mean it. I figured I have your full attention right now so it was a good time to bring it up." Her mouth brushed his. "I ache for you. Will you make love to me slowly? I want to savor every second of having you inside me."

"Slow next time. I need you," he rasped, lifting her hips and slamming her back down onto him, thrusting every inch of his hard flesh inside her.

His strength turned her on as he lifted her and pulled her down, helping her ride him fast and hard. Pure rapture spread through her body with every movement, every up-and-down glide of her body on his, and their breathing turned choppy as they moved faster together, frantically trying to reach climax. The pleasure increased with the speed until it became nearly unbearable for Megan. Her inner vaginal walls clenched, gripping him tighter, and then she screamed, coming hard.

Ice's body arched under hers, his back leaving the padded floor, and he threw back his head as Megan's muscles milked his cock, sending him over the edge with her as he roared her name.

"Warning," the computer voice suddenly spoke. "Oxygen consumption over the safety limit. Life forms in danger."

Ice jerked, his head lowering. "What is that? Who is that?"

Megan grinned, panting, and opened her mouth to explain about the onboard computer but she suddenly felt lightheaded. Her grin died as she realized what had happened. She saw Ice's eyes widen with alarm and then she collapsed on his chest. His body turned limp under hers and his hands dropped away from her hips.

The computer had gassed them to knock them out, thinking they were unruly passengers who needed to be calmed. Megan tried to fight passing out but the chemicals worked fast. Blackness rushed at her as she lost consciousness.

Chapter Fourteen

"That should do it. Should we lift her off him?"

Those were the first words Megan heard as she started to come around. The drugs the computer had used to subdue her and Ice would leave them sluggish and a little out of it until they wore off. She remembered what had happened and tried to make sense of why she heard male voices instead of the automated, computer one. She had to be dreaming or imagining things. Her eyes opened and she stared at the padding on the side of the capsule.

The bright light made her want to groan. For some reason they'd been put on full bright, and she sprawled on top of Ice. Her cheek rested over his heart and her arms were stretched above her over his shoulders, her hands loosely curled next to his warm neck. Under her, Ice stirred, a soft groan coming from him, and inside her, his cock twitched. They were still physically connected.

"Drugged," he groaned.

"I know." She rubbed her cheek against his warm chest. Her skin tingled, another side effect from the gas they'd been exposed to. "The computer probably thought we were freaking out and triggered the drugs to calm us down."

His arm moved and Megan realized that Ice was wiping her hair away from his face. He blew out air and then turned his head. She lifted hers and stared down into his sleepy, sexy eyes. She smiled.

"Calmer now? How did I do, getting a handle on your fear? I'm hoping you have another panic attack. I could totally go another round."

He smiled and then his gaze shifted from hers to something behind her. His smile died and she watched his beautiful gray skin pale until he nearly turned a milky white. Whatever he saw alarmed her. Had something gone wrong when she'd hit her head on the lid? There were some control functions there. She jerked her head around to follow his stare.

The lid stood open and she wasn't staring at a set of controls. She saw metal beams far above her and two cyborg males were standing over them, both smiling, and she knew one of them. Flint winked.

"Hello. I'm glad that you are with us again. We hoped the oxygen would revive you when we opened the lid. You were both unconscious." Flint arched an eyebrow. "We'll back away while you fix your clothing." His gaze lowered down Megan's body and he chuckled. "And put pants on."

Heat flamed Megan's cheeks, realizing that she straddled Ice, her body naked from the waist down. She sat up slowly, afraid to move off him, and peered over the edge of the open capsule. She recognized the cargo bay of the *Star* immediately and saw a group of cyborgs standing about ten feet away with their backs turned. Four other capsules were taking up space on the floor near them.

"We're on the *Star*," Ice stated.

"I know." She slowly eased off his hips, embarrassment still warming her cheeks as they separated, and she lifted up enough for Ice's cock to totally withdraw from her body. "Shit. They just saw my ass," she whispered.

"You have a very attractive one." Ice chuckled.

Her gaze lowered as she frantically reached back, feeling for her discarded pants. So, he found the situation funny. She sure didn't. She eased completely off him and he pulled his pants up, covered his flaccid cock, and fastened his pants. He sat up and pulled his legs out of her way. She sat up, yanked on her pants, and kept low so no one could see her movements. Ice climbed out by using the edges to lift up and swing a leg over the rim of the capsule.

Megan fastened her pants and then Ice bent over her, one arm hooking under the back of her knees while his other one wrapped around her waist. When he lifted her, she wrapped her arms around his neck as he straightened, turned, and then gently set her on her bare feet on the deck of the cargo bay.

Flint turned and walked close again, his humor gone and his expression tense. "Now that you're alert, where is Councilman Zorus? We recovered three council members and Roan. They had reprogrammed the computers by remote linking and hacking the pods to head back to this ship and signaled us to meet them when they were within range. We immediately traced the path of the enemy shuttle and found your pod floating dead in space." He paused. "Why didn't you reprogram your pod to reach us?"

A sheepish expression crossed Ice's features. "I wasn't aware of the onboard computer until it made its presence known seconds before it gassed us. I was distracted."

"You decided to have sex." Amusement had Flint grinning.

234

"I had an episode." Ice glanced at Megan and sighed. "I know I need to address my issues with tight spaces. Luckily Megan kept me from panicking. It seems sex overrides my fear."

Flint turned serious. "The sixth pod hasn't been located. Did it deploy? The shuttle from Earth blew up into large pieces that we found scattered in space. We checked the debris field but did not find it or his body but it was a mass of objects, too many and too tightly compacted to search. It's possible we missed it. The council is very agitated to discover the fate of Zorus."

Ice opened his mouth but before he could talk, Megan stepped forward to draw Flint's attention.

"Zorus and Coal are out there somewhere in the sixth capsule. We have to find them."

"I don't understand why Zorus didn't link to and reprogram the computer to pilot him toward my ship, as the others did. We were scanning as we looked for you and did not find them." He paused. "Coal is with him? I thought he returned to the *Rally*."

"Um," Megan swallowed the lump that formed in her throat. "Zorus was out cold. He, um, hit his head. Would Coal have reprogrammed the capsule to return to the *Rally*? Maybe that's where he's heading."

"Zorus has been injured?"

Ice sighed. "He was after I hit him."

Megan winced. Why had he admitted that? Would he be in trouble? Worry ate at her as she darted a glance at Flint, seeing his dark eyebrows rise in reaction to that information.

"You struck him?"

"He ordered me to leave Megan behind to die."

Flint's gaze hardened. "I would have punched him as well if he ordered me to abandon my wife."

"I do not know where he is. Coal struck me when I ordered him and Megan to take the last two capsules. I had planned to stay behind with Zorus on the enemy shuttle."

"Coal told me he would put them both into the last one," Megan said softly. "He wanted them to have a chance at survival. We could smell wires burning and he said the fire had reached the conduits inside the walls and he thought life support would fail at any time."

A loud sigh escaped Flint. "I will inform the council that we have no idea what happened. I'll contact the *Rally* and have them backtrack to our location and scan for them. We'll start a search grid and attempt to locate that capsule." He fixed his full attention on Megan. "Did they launch before you did or after?"

"After. Coal sealed the lid on the capsule Ice and I were in. The last I saw of him, he stood over me, but I know he planned to put himself and Zorus into the other one."

Another cyborg approached. Megan did a double take when he did. He had the silver-gray hair that came with old age but his face contradicted that. He didn't look a day over thirty-five. His bright-blue eyes drew her attention and held it. The unusual color was so pale and blue they nearly glowed. For a second, she wondered if he was blind. He gave her a tight smile, glancing directly at her, and then met Ice's gaze.

"They may not have had a chance to escape." He had a really unusual voice with its gruff, raspy tone.

Flint nodded, his expression grim. "The explosion that destroyed the Earth shuttle was severe. We'll do an extensive search, cover the area, and if we don't find them we'll assume they didn't survive." He addressed the cyborg with the strangely beautiful eyes. "I'm off shift so it's all yours, Sky."

Ice wrapped an arm around Megan, pulling her to his side. "What of the Markus Models?"

"We saw one of them drifting in space." Sky shook his head. "It survived the blast. It attempted to wave its arms to flag us down to pull it inside our ship. It was creepy as hell to see it and I hope to never do so again. They really appear human. Seeing him floating out there, moving around, was freakish, and then to top it off, he attempted to throw small debris items at the *Star* to get our attention, as if we weren't aware of him."

Ice's body tensed. "You brought it inside the *Star*?"

The large cyborg shook his head. "Hell no. We left it out there. It can drift in space until it uses up all its battery power or something slams into it. I'm hoping a big asteroid smashes it into tiny pieces. They are not allies, and with Zorus not here to demand we do otherwise, we decided it wasn't worth the risk. They wanted to turn us over to Earth Government so it can kiss my ass. It's lucky I didn't think it was worth some target practice."

Flint chuckled. "I'm glad to have you back, Sky. I've missed your unique assessment of matters."

Ice chuckled. "Sky is our Earth expert. He was assigned by the council to listen in on all Earth vessel transmissions. He tends to speak as they do and take on some of their traits."

"He has picked up of their amusing language." Flint grinned. "Kiss your ass? Really? I hope that's not a literal statement."

"Bite me." Sky grinned. "And no, not literal." His gaze lowered to Megan. "You're hot, babe. Ever done a cyborg?"

Ice tugged Megan tighter against his side. "She's my wife."

Sky's grin died. "Sorry. I wasn't informed you'd joined a family unit. I had hoped you'd rescued her from the Earth shuttle and she happened to be an unattached female. I'd love to possess one of my own." He laughed suddenly. "To help with my language skills, of course." He winked.

Flint chuckled. "If you'd arrived in the cargo bay a few minutes earlier when we opened the capsule you wouldn't have had to ask if she's familiar with a cyborg male."

Megan's cheeks burned and Ice shook his head. "Stop teasing my female." He hesitated. "Is there anything I can do to help with the search? I can take Megan to my quarters and settle her there before reporting for duty."

"I have it." Sky shifted his stance. "How hard do I really have to look for Zorus? He's not my favorite person. He ordered me into his special project, and let me assure you, I haven't enjoyed being stuck on Garden with his uppity attitude. As soon as we find him, he's going to drag my ass back there. The only reason I'm here is because he thought I might be of use with those freaky machines that can pass for human. I am in no hurry to go back or have him barking out orders at me. The guy is a first rate asshole."

Flint hesitated.

"Coal is with him," Ice reminded them.

"Got it." Sky muttered something under his breath. "Poor sucker. I feel sorry for anyone stuck with Zorus." He turned on his heel and marched away.

Flint smiled, watching Sky leave the cargo bay, and then turned to face Ice. "It wouldn't be a tragedy if Zorus didn't survive." His smile faded. "Coal, on the other hand, would be a loss. I like him, though we've only briefly known him."

"Hopefully they escaped the shuttle before it blew."

"Hopefully. You've survived an ordeal. Take your wife to your quarters and I'll have some food sent to you. Relax. I'll tell Sky to inform you of the results of the search."

"Thank you for picking us up."

Flint studied him. "I'm surprised you're alive and didn't fight your way out of that tiny life pod. I know you have issues with being enclosed in small spaces."

"Megan kept me calm."

"Is that what she was doing on top of you? When my wife is half naked, sitting on my lap, I'm anything but calm." Flint grinned.

"Funny." Megan shook her head at the two smiling men, seeing their shared amusement at the joke. "I'm more than ready to get out of this outfit."

"You were just out of half of it," Flint pointed out, chuckling.

Ice laughed, tugging at Megan. "I don't believe she's amused by our teasing. She doesn't enjoying the weight of the uniform I gave her. We'll be in my quarters. The *Rally* is great but it's tighter on space and as you mentioned, more is my preference. I'll be happy to spend time in my quarters here."

"I am glad that you survived." Flint moved away, walking toward the cyborgs who were moving the capsules to the side of the bay, clearing the center of the large room.

"Come with me," Ice ordered softly, releasing her waist as he offered her his arm.

She gripped it and walked beside him. Five minutes later they entered his living space on the *Star*. "Nice. It's about ten feet bigger than your other one."

"Yes. I do enjoy commanding the *Rally* but I mainly live here." He paused. "I'll put in a request for larger quarters. They have them for the males in a family unit who have their female travel with them."

Megan watched Ice remove his clothing. She hesitated and then stripped out of the uncomfortable uniform, planning to take a foam cleansing. Her thoughts were on the cyborg who had saved their lives and what it would mean if Zorus hadn't survived.

"What is wrong?"

She lifted her chin. "I was just thinking about Zorus and Coal."

He closed the distance between them and peered down at her. "You have a worried expression. They might have survived."

"Zorus is the one who hates humans and the one who really pushed for that vote for everyone to decide to kill me, right?"

"He swung the council's vote that way. He makes no secret of his hatred of humans."

"If he died..." She hesitated.

"What is it? I won't be in any trouble, Megan. No one will hold me accountable for his death."

"That's good to know and half of my worry just left."

"Half?"

"If he's dead, does that mean you don't have to be in a family unit with me any longer to keep them from killing me?"

A tinge of anger showed on Ice's features. "We are a family unit and his fate has no consequence on that."

"I want to know the answer. If he's dead, do you have to be in a family unit to keep them from ordering me killed in the future?"

He gripped her hips and jerked her hard against his naked body. It surprised Megan. She gripped his upper arms as she watched him glare at her. He lifted her high enough that her feet left the floor and she rose until they were face level.

"You're mine and even if you aren't willing to accept it, that is your fate. I will not release you from the contract." He paused. "Ever."

241

Staring into his beautiful silvery-blue eyes, she swallowed. He looked so angry it stunned her. "I—"

"Belong to me. You're mine, have been mine since the moment you asked me how you could serve me. I gave you the opportunity to stop what was happening between us but you allowed me into your body and then you asked to stay in my quarters with me to keep you alive." He paused. "You already know I have feelings for you. Do you think they would change just because it's no longer a necessity to keep you safe from the council's orders?"

"I also know that you didn't want to join a family unit. You didn't want to get attached. If Zorus is dead then the option is there for you again. Nothing is stopping you from just walking away from me."

"Have your feelings for me changed, Megan? Do you want me to release you?"

"No." She wouldn't lie to him. "I am worried if Zorus died that you might *want* to release me. I realize you probably felt you had to go that far to protect me and now there will no longer be a reason if that guy died."

Ice took a deep breath, his chest pressing tightly against hers. "There's a reason."

"Will someone else on the council insist I'm dangerous?"

In a heartbeat Ice's mouth covered Megan's, his full, strong lips forcing hers apart, and his tongue forged inside. Surprise held her immobile for a few seconds and then she kissed him back. Her hands slid up his arms and wrapped around his neck. The passion flared brightly between them as the kiss deepened.

Ice broke their lips apart, both of them breathing heavily, and his intense gaze locked with hers. He moved them toward the foam cleansing unit but neither spoke. His arm wrapped around her waist, securing her to his body as he reached out to hit the button to lower the wall.

"You're my female, we're a family unit, and what we feel is reason enough to never allow you to leave me."

She hesitated, chewing on her bottom lip, and knew he had to see the tears that filled her eyes. "Everyone has always abandoned me, Ice. My mom did it and then my dad just took off when he deemed me old enough to make it on my own. It hurt me deeply inside and I've kept people distanced from me emotionally ever since. I don't want to ever wake up one day and watch you walk away from me too. It would kill me. Don't say those things unless you really mean them. Don't make me believe you and one day break my heart."

His features softened as he stared into her eyes. One hand lifted as he adjusted her in his arms to cup her face in his big palm. "We've both known so much pain and loneliness in our lives." He drew closer. "You are never going to be without me. We are one unit now and that will never change." His lips brushed hers but he didn't deepen the kiss. He pulled back instead. "We'll even expand our family unit."

Her eyebrows rose.

"I believe sharing our DNA will strengthen our bond and heal the hurt we've both suffered."

"Are you talking about children?"

He grinned. "Yes."

"Couldn't you just say that? Shared DNA?" She grinned and started to tease him. "Okay. Want to have *intercourse* now, tall, gray, and sexy?"

He chuckled. "No. I want to fuck you and afterward, I want to make love to you slowly in our bed."

She nodded. "I want that too. I just needed to be sure you wouldn't one day feel resentment from being pushed into starting a family unit with me, Ice."

"Baby, out of all the things I'm feeling, that is not one of the emotions I'm experiencing. You've taught me to love. I'll teach you that what we have will last and we'll share both of those things with the children we create together." He pressed her back to the wall. "Close your eyes." His arm moved as he reached to activate the foam.

Megan closed her eyes and in seconds foam coated them. Her skin tingled all over as it worked, cleaning them and then slowly melting into water drops that slid down her skin. Her eyes opened only to find Ice watching her.

"I love you and I refuse to allow you to leave me. Deal with that."

Happiness surrounded her, along with the love that centered on the sexy man in front of her. "You're so bossy but okay. I'll do that." She lifted her legs, wrapped them around his hips, and her ankles crossed over his ass. "How may I serve you?"

Gorgeous silvery-blue eyes widened and then his sexy, full lips curved into a grin. "I can think of many, many ways, my little sex bot."

Laughing, she winked at him and then tilted her head, going for the side of his neck. She licked his skin and then lightly raked her teeth there before kissing him. Her tongue traced up to just under his earlobe.

"Tell me to wiggle my hips so you can enter me and take me right here, right now, against this wall. I want you."

"I give the orders."

"I know. So tell me to do what I just said."

He laughed. "Life will never be boring with you, will it?"

She nibbled his ear. "No. Definitely not, tall, gray and sexy."

Ice's hips shifted and his hard cock pressed against her entrance. He slowly lowered her until his cock rested deep inside her pussy. He froze there. Megan was wet and ready for him, aching, and as he slid into her, she turned her head. Their gazes locked.

"I love you," Ice whispered. "You make me feel everything."

"I love you too." Megan wiggled her hips. "Now I want to feel everything, as in move. You're torturing me. You're throbbing inside me."

"So demanding," he chuckled.

Ice slowly withdrew his cock almost totally out of her welcoming depths only to drive back up inside her. Their bodies moved together, skin to skin, lips to lips. In minutes they both were crying out the other's name.

"I know how heaven must feel," he groaned. "You've given me that."

"I got the one thing I wanted most." Her fingers gripped his shoulders as their gazes locked together. "I got you."

"You've got me and we belong to each other."

* * * * *

A buzz woke Ice. He opened his eyes and smiled when he realized that Megan sprawled on top of his body, her cheek over his heart and her legs on the outside of his. The buzz sounded again. He was tempted to ignore it but the person at his door refused to stop pressing for his attention.

He gently rolled until Megan settled on her side. She muttered something in her sleep but didn't wake. He carefully got off his bed, covered her bare body, and then moved to the drawers. He just pulled on shorts before he opened the door. Onyx stood there.

Ice stepped out into the hallway, allowing the door to close behind him so their conversation didn't wake his wife. He wanted her well rested. He studied his longtime friend and saw sadness in his eyes.

"I attempted to link with you to avoid coming to your door but you have your com link off."

"I was sleeping with Megan." He paused. "Obviously the *Rally* is docked with the *Star* since you are here."

Nodding, Onyx blew out a breath. "We can't find the life capsule. We had no choice but to deem it destroyed with the enemy shuttle. We assume they did not have a chance to launch away."

"Damn." Ice's shoulders slumped. "Poor Coal. He survived all those years trapped with cyborg females who abused him, finally had his freedom, only to lose his life now. That is just unacceptable."

"Not to mention that he died with Zorus. That is not a face I would want to see in my last moments of life."

"At least Zorus won't be a threat to my Megan anymore."

Onyx studied him and then cursed. "Damn it."

"What?"

"You have that same happy look that Flint, Steel, and Iron have when they talk about their females. Are human women that good in bed?"

Ice hesitated. "It's more than the sex, my friend. Megan makes me forget what I am and allows me to be who I always aspired to be. Do you understand? I'm not a cyborg to her but instead just a man. A man who is very happy that she changed my life. For the first time in my existence, I feel alive. I feel true rightness." He paused. "I am complete."

"I still don't believe any female is worth the trouble they cause."

"Megan is worth everything to me."

"I'm returning to the *Rally*." Onyx backed up. "I enjoy not having one to tell me what to do."

"You'd be surprised how pleasurable some orders are that she gives me." He laughed, remembering Megan's demands in the shower. "I'll see you on my next shift."

Ice entered his quarters and paused to watch the woman sleeping in his bed. He loved her and finally knew the meaning of being truly alive. She'd said love was a gift and now he understood. He yanked off his shorts, got into bed, and then pulled his woman into his arms, where she belonged.

25825903R00148

Printed in Poland
by Amazon Fulfillment
Poland Sp. z o.o., Wrocław